Queer Africa

new and collected fiction

Queer Africa

new and collected fiction

EDITED BY KAREN MARTIN AND MAKHOSAZANA XABA

First published in 2013 by MaThoko's Books
PO Box 31719, Braamfontein, 2017, South Africa

ISBN: 978-1-920590-33-8

Cover art: Carla Kreuser
Book and cover design: Monique Cleghorn

Printed and bound by Creda Communications, Cape Town

Set in 11 pt on 15 pt Adobe Caslon

MaThoko's Books is an imprint of Gay and Lesbian Memory in Action (GALA).

The
ATLANTIC
Philanthropies

The publication of this book was made possible by core support
from The Atlantic Philanthropies.

CONTENTS

Queer Africa is a collection of charged, tangled, tender, unapologetic, funny, bruising and brilliant stories about the many ways in which we love one another on the continent. The collection includes exquisitely written work by some of the great African writers of this century – K. Sello Duiker, Monica Arac de Nyeko, Beatrice Lamwaka and Richard de Nooy – as well as new voices that map out a haunting, intricate, complex Africa. Phrases like Wamuwi Mbao's 'She looks like you, when nobody's watching her' and Sello Duiker's narrator's 'gentle sadness that doesn't take you all at once' share with us not only the aftermath of sex, but moments where the world opens itself. In these unafraid stories of intimacy, sweat, betrayal and restless confidences, we accompany characters into cafes, tattoo salons, the barest of bedrooms, the coldly glinting spaces into which the rich withdraw, unlit streets, and their own deepest interiors. We learn much in these gloriously achieved stories about love and sex, but perhaps more about why we hurt and need one another.

– GABEBA BADEROON

PREFACE

The arts allow us to consider experiences radically different from our own in ways that other forms of representation (research reports, the media, etc.) can't. In imaginative space, dominant narratives hold less sway; possibilities we haven't considered suggest themselves. We are confronted with our prejudices and preconceptions. And we may discover in others our own unrecognised selves. It is our intention with this anthology to productively disrupt, through the art of literature, the potent discourses currently circulating on what it means to be African, to be queer and to be an African creative writer.

One of the earliest conversations we had with GALA was about how we could capture the widest range of stories – female and male, cis- and trans-gender, urban and rural, contemporary and historical, joyful and troubled – without compromising literary values. In a later discussion, we committed to our interest in how a range of writers might respond to and represent queer Africa by deciding that writers need not identify as queer to qualify for the anthology. We did stipulate that writers must identify as African, and we allowed them to decide for themselves what this means. We are proud now to showcase diverse writers from the African creative writing community, reflecting and imagining for us the kaleidoscopic variety of queer lives on our continent.

Queer Africa: New and Collected Fiction celebrates the diversity and fluidity of queer and African identifications and expressions. For instance, it features a number of stories about queer men written by women, and by men about queer women. Indeed, many stories ignore the national, gender and racial identity boundaries of their writers. These writers have made courageous literary journeys, and their stories challenge assumptions about what it means to legitimately represent a particular human experience. Something else we like about the anthology is that some of the stories renew over-represented aspects of African life by looking at them through a queer lens. "Chief of the Home", one of the highlights of the collection, examines conflict in semi-rural Uganda from the perspective of a trans protagonist. It is neither a war story nor a trans story, but a unique queer space in which to consider the impact of violent conflict on individuals.

When making our final selections we decided to include some previously published stories. This not only allowed us to provide a wider range of content but also to feature stories from more countries. But still, *Queer Africa*'s geographic range is limited. On the one hand, our publicity was constrained by time and money. On the other, we were puzzled by limited responses from some of the writing communities we did reach out to. We are pleased, though, that including these previously published stories – some of them widely celebrated, like "Jambula Tree" – allows them to be re-read in a context that foregrounds their queerness.

It has taken three years to collect and assemble the anthology. What sort of queer, African, literary and advocacy space is it entering in 2013? In parts of Africa, stronger and stronger queer voices are making themselves heard – the voices of activists and artists, of communities and politicians. In other parts, terrifying violence, often sanctioned by the state, plagues queer people. *Queer Africa* will confront the noisy political rhetoric that positions queerness as unnatural, amoral and un-African with intimate stories about individual lives, deeply embedded in the complexities of their contexts, and crafted by some of Africa's finest writers.

May you be provoked and inspired by the queer African imaginings we bring you here.

— KAREN MARTIN AND MAKHOSAZANA XABA
JOHANNESBURG, MARCH 2013

INTRODUCTION

Karen Martin and Makhosazana Xaba have achieved an extraordinary feat in bringing together this very welcome volume of stories that imagine queer Africa in such diverse and exciting ways. It is a beautiful and necessary project that presents a shared vision across the pages of the book whilst allowing the individual short stories, and the two excerpts from novels, to stand completely in their own stead. A shared vision is not premised on agreement or similarity, as these stories show; the editors of the collection gesture towards a political, aesthetic and imaginative community that is not premised on sameness. After all, each of these stories offers a slice of what it means to be queer in Africa because, in a direct sense, that description and call were what the authors responded to or what their stories suggested, prompting invitations to publish here.

One of the implied questions in this volume that is sometimes directly addressed, and obliquely gestured towards at other times, is the exact meaning of "queer" when it rubs up against "Africa". The stories themselves show the very many ways in which being queer in Africa, a queer Africa and queering Africa are not the same thing across time, borders, and internal boundaries, even as we read "queer" as always concerned with identity and a deliberate perspective in/on the world. The framing of this anthology in these terms brings together a range of world narratives about shared sexual, gender and political identification. *Queer Africa*, as a name for this collection, also comes with the many ways in which "queer" is equally embraced and questioned by those it seeks to include and/or speak on behalf of. In a very direct sense, here we have what Gabeba Baderoon has called a "leaking of meaning", producing not a tidy putting together, but sometimes a coherent sense of belonging, and at other times a provisional one. Meaning leaks here because the many discussions and debates on the use of queer in African contexts are varied and on-going. These debates have the discoveries, frustrations, excitement and anger that come with all politically difficult conversations worth having. While some use the label comfortably, others are worried about whether it adequately speaks usefully to contexts outside the geographical politics of its emergence. Does its use give credence to or help challenge the homophobic claims of importation? Does it contest African hegemonies by using terms of reference that come from a place that paid no attention to queer his/her/hirstories on the continent? Others use it selectively and carefully, as shorthand, or under erasure, depending on what political work they are invested in doing across temporalities and geographies. As I continue to use "queer" in this introduction, I do so mindful of these contradictions and questions. I also use it as someone whose own self-identification does not stand outside of this embattlement, and no amount of quoting Judith Butler even begins to address the problem. I write also aware that there are probably as many "queers" who use it interchangeably with LGTBI as there are who insist on the two meaning very different things. Some of these difficulties can be glimpsed in *Queer African Reader*, edited by Sokari Ekine and Hakima Abbas, as well as in Hakima Abbas and Jessica Horn's Movement Building Boot Camp for Queer African Activists. These are not the only places.

Let me return more directly to the stories.

Read separately, these narratives offer testimony to the universality/multiversality of queer subjects and imaginations, as they invite the readers to leave no historic, religious, contemporary or geographic landscape untouched. They are a powerful response to the conservative dismissal of LGBTI histories and presences on the African continent as foreign, decadent importations. In the stories gathered here, we see love, excitement, joy, heartbreak, transcendence, sorrow and a range of other feelings and experiences that make up the very fibre of all human life.

Read collectively, the stories go beyond simply showing how it is possible to imagine queer expression on any landscape. It is not an additive, inclusive vision proposed here, but one that takes the queer imagination seriously as a lens through which to view the macro political and the intimate, always at the same time. Yes, the personal is political here too, and nothing is more political than love for those brutalised and systematically erased. In order to give life to such politics, the stories need not share a philosophy of representation, or indeed occupy the same ideological position on any other area. The conversations that occur across stories can be difficult ones because in the same volume you have the collision of vastly different conceptual universes. This makes for some unpredictable reading, since some stories delight and others frighten, depending on who the reader is. I will not say that there is something for everyone in this collection – that is not what variety, conversation, difference and friction mean.

As a collection, *Queer Africa: New and Collected Fiction* brings together a range of voices, colours, strengths and ambiguities. There are some things to be expected, but between these covers lies enchantment and heartbreak too. The stories do not span the entire continent and the collection makes no claim to that kind of representivity. East and Southern Africa dominate, and within Southern Africa, there are further raced, class, and geographical amplifications.

Intersections of gender and/or sexual identity with race, class and colonial/apartheid violence is more explicitly present in stories like Rahiem Whisgary's "The Filth of Freedom", which is also about the intertwining of pain, race and entitlement. We see a similar register in an otherwise differently toned "Leaving Civvy Street" by Annie Holmes, which treats these themes through anxiety, power, fear and inner turmoil.

"Pinch" and "Poisoned Grief" are imaginative cousins. Emil Rorke's "Poisoned Grief" captures enmeshed danger and discovery in a hostile world that will not see two men's desire for each other, much like Monica Arac de Nyeko's story that I discuss below. Meiring and Ludolf are placed, by Martin Hatchuel, in the context of Afrikaner-English warfare, where the impending danger of discovery, deception and reception are as ever-present as the mutual desire. In these stories lies the important insistence on claiming history as always already also queer. It is not an insertion of desire in key historical moments that is undertaken here. Rather, such moments are re-examined from a lens that asks what a queer experience might have looked like in that moment. It is one queer experience among many other possibilities. Even as the story captures the specific well, it also acts to suggest infinite other possibilities.

The most heart-wrenching story in this collection is presented in the most elegant prose. Wamuwi Mbao's "The Bath" is a deceptively short but rich and layered story. Each page is pain-soaked, as the narrator takes us through the hopelessness and futile suicide attempts after the loss of a loved one. This is such wonderful writing that I can barely wait to see what else Mbao has in store for readers.

Another beautifully written painful encounter comes in an extract from a novel. Uninterested in the simplifying gaze, Richard de Nooy's story in this collection is simultaneously beautiful and painful. In it, he grasps at fluidity whilst embracing uncertainty and movement. De Nooy's sympathetic narrator centres Princess so that s/he is the one who makes sense while the others are slightly out of focus. This is a story about value, aesthetics and seeing differently.

Perspective is revisited so differently in this anthology that it seems a disservice to even classify these stories as dealing with "ways of seeing". In To Molefe's "Lower Main", as in the excerpt from K. Sello Duiker's brilliant *Thirteen Cents*, we see a Cape Town often obscured from view, given the privileging of the tourist gaze. These stories both return to articulate differently. Molefe's narrator's Cape Town emerges through competing languages of desire whilst negotiating what cannot or should not be desired. This story is about so much more than playing with bodies in an exploration of identity; it is also about what it means to be a subject who is constantly observed, read, consumed and packaged by some other gaze owned by those who have no consideration for your own self-making. Molefe's central characters are not defined by this gaze even as they cannot escape it. Madz's and TeeKay's very names foreground experimentation and play, something that exists in the architecture of Molefe's story.

In Wame Molefhe's "Sethunya Likes Girls Better", the author probes the regimes of femininity with always assumed and enforced heterosexuality, the masking and patterns of empathy and identification. Such knotty and heavy matters are nonetheless rendered in Molefhe's prose as a story of hope, ambivalence and beauty in the midst of it all.

If art is supposed to unsettle alongside its many other roles of illuminating, probing, tickling and theorising the world, then Mercy Minah's "In the Way She Glides" offered the most challenge to me as a reader. This is a story that makes for increasingly uncomfortable reading. Centring on the places of desire in the competitive world of school sports, offering multiple backstories of desire, coupling and uncoupling, it also flirts with the borderline-problematic gentle arousal of a teacher as she watches a student she coaches. Even on re-reading, this story troubled me in ways I cannot fully articulate without spoiling the story for those readers who will come to this collection initially through this introduction. I remain least convinced by its vision.

On the other hand, I found Natasha Distiller's story "Asking for It" refreshing. In this provocatively titled story, the author returns to something we find elsewhere in her writing: the investment in developing a language of the body, beauty and love. The two characters develop a vocabulary that is at once exclusively theirs and Julia's. We are invited to pause on the process of becoming for Cath, as Distiller blends the attractive into the burdensome.

Queer Africa: New and Collected Fiction is multi-vocal and multiversal. It blends established, groundbreaking stories, like Sello Duiker's and Arac de Nyeko's exquisite, award-winning "Jambula Tree", with more careful, delicate narratives. While visibility and ways of seeing are everywhere in this volume, there is an expansion of the phrase "what you see when you look at me", to borrow from Zanele Muholi's work. Here, like in Muholi's work, there is less focus on queer Africa moving into the line of vision from "invisibility" and more emphasis on seeing differently, offering a new toolkit for representation.

Arac de Nyeko's short story uses the gentlest, sexy and exquisite prose to speak about desire and growth. It is about how two girls growing into women fall in love in the most logical and illogical of ways. This journey into mutual adoration is the most natural thing in the world, as Arac de Nyeko reminds us. I read it slowly, savouring every word, even on this one of multiple re-readings.

I could not help thinking of Dolar Vasani's "All Covered Up" as a story in similar terrain, even if the contents of these two stories could not be more different. Vasani's is a beautiful, sensual narrative that is at the same time incredibly political in what is disrupted, played around with and teased out. Drawing out a sexy, sensual encounter across religion, where barriers are both as large as a world and as thin as a *buibui*, the author offers a gift of a story where seduction is an art, as is the reading of fully clothed bodies.

Reading Davina Owombre's "Pelican Driver" offers another encounter with the sexy, this time coupled with risk. Located within a language of a pop culture both ambivalent and deceptively simple in its engagement of sexuality and gender, the writer makes space for desire and sex in an otherwise clearly bounded aesthetic space. Here we are witness to, and pulled into the transgression of, desire: masking, performing, playing in a story in which humour and risk are twinned.

Individually and collectively, the stories in *Queer Africa: New and Collected Fiction* differ in what is uncovered and questioned, what is taken for granted and that which is imagined anew. As I bring this introduction to a close, I turn to the most delightful story in the collection: Beatrice Lamwaka's "Chief of the Home".

In this loving tribute, the writer stages the reclamation of a loved one rejected for being himself. Here, Lamwaka tells the story of Lugul with deep appreciation for his "deviant" masculinity and his freedom as deliberate self-identification. Yet, it is a story that reclaims without exaggerating its dues. In the embrace, there is no closure, no absolute clarity.

Lamwaka's "Chief of the Home" is a love story in the most radical meaning of that phrase: a loving insistence on recovering the most frightening and rejected part of the self. It is an insistence on valuing what makes her narrator feel good as a child and an adult. It is a return to love, as a radical revision of the world and as a gift to self. In many ways, this is also a description of this volume. I hope it is a gift to all of us, whether we ever, always or sometimes call ourselves queer.

– PUMLA DINEO GQOLA

PELICAN DRIVER

DAVINA OWOMBRE

AJ got off his knees, licking his lips. He inhaled with gusto and flexed his wings. Even if he revved up this party for two with an old school anthem, his high couldn't get any higher.

He bobbed his dreadlocks to an imaginary beat. Might as well enjoy it, he thought. Tweeshock's *Shame On Me* video would premiere on Channel O the next day. It didn't matter that his scene barely lasted two heartbeats. Everybody would see two men smooching; his twin sister Antonia would recognise him: and she would not high-five him when she did.

Still nodding to the beat in his head, AJ sank into his producer's chair – which now backed the digital console instead of facing it – and watched Louis walking away, tugging up the zip on his trousers. The soft grating whispered through the room before the opening door whooshed away the sound. Closing, the door inadvertently cut off AJ's imaginary beat. He swung round and glared beyond the glass partition. The recording booth stood empty, the mike a soundless witness at the centre of the soundproof room.

He exhaled. These quick sessions with Louis didn't bother him. Hell, he enjoyed giving Louis blowjobs: the tangy-salty taste of cum in his mouth still thrilled him – as if he were a first timer. How they always forgot to make sure they were alone, baffled him. The studio often had people passing through. Why did they risk getting caught?

The answer, a thumping, kick drum of sudden clarity, thudded at his chest and made him stop: perhaps they wanted to get caught.

He chuckled and reached across the console with a long, thin finger. He pushed the playback button, turning on the track he'd been working on before Louis walked in. The music – motor noise without rhythm – filled the studio. Kick drums and snare drums followed a universal hip-hop pattern, with bass guitar leading a banjo through regular loops and a hang-in-there riff. So what if he got caught with his boss? Anybody who knew Louis enough to saunter into the studio whenever they liked, probably already knew he swung both ways. Since AJ liked his job and didn't dislike his fun-seeking music promoter boss, he didn't care what people thought of him.

He cared what got back to Antonia though, and the smooching scene in *Shame On Me* would only give bite to her recent charge that they were now strangers just sharing a flat. He hissed and hit the stop button. The sudden silence smelled of loneliness. Antonia deserved to hear the truth from him regardless of how she would take it.

He slapped off the lights and grabbed his bag. No point wasting Friday night trying to salvage what had been doomed from conception. How could a hopeless song with a title like "Come Out and Dance" fire anyone's creativity? Look at Tweeshock's "Shame On Me", which AJ'd produced. Now there's a song that rocks, he thought. That he'd been asked to appear in the video proved Tweeshock loved his work.

Waiting to catch a taxi home, the mood took him: "I'm primitive / My poetry must have some true rhymes / Not definitive? / Well, I'm not syncing with the times / You're looking badly beaten, were you married to Ike Turner? / Just go back to *your* corner and let me hide up in *my* corner / Don't want to see your tears / They remind me of my fears / Shame on me / Shame on you / Shame on us!"

Home hid in the darkness of Abuja's Gwarimpa district, a quarter still burgeoning in the dry season of 2009. The electricity had gone off again and several power generators roaring in the area gave it the ambience of a noisy industrial complex. His big-assed neighbour Pat sat on the steps in a short skirt. She puffed a cancer stick. The resulting smoke created a light haziness about her usually well made-up face. Like AJ and Antonia, Pat had one of the twelve, self-contained, one-bedroom flats in their one storey building.

"AJ Slim," Pat smiled. "You're back early today."

AJ smiled back and caressed Pat's outstretched palm. He figured Pat could be three or four years older than him. She always played the v cool elder sister. And though she had a body that would still ooze sex even if a prudish monk draped a tattered sack over her, he'd taken to pretending brotherly love.

He pointed at her cigarette. "You don't read the Ministry of Health's warning?"

Pat doused him with smoke from her nostrils. "'All that live will die,' says the Bible."

"Does it? I failed Bible Knowledge. You stopped shooting for overtime pay?"

Pat made space for him on her step. "The not-for-profits are gathering in Paris for another funding jamboree. My bastard boss chose to go alone. How's the studio?"

"I'm cooking beats for a set of songs so bad they're goats with glued-on wings."

Pat gave him a playful push. "Can't be that bad."

AJ shrugged. "No one's ever heard of the guy. He can't sing to save his life. Yet he's insisting on titling his first single 'Pelican Driver', just because it's his stage name."

Pat tried to laugh but ended up coughing. AJ patted her on the back and signalled that he wanted a puff from her cigarette. Surprised, Pat shared the cigarette. "You smoke?"

AJ inhaled. He didn't really smoke, but the rhythm of pleasure hadn't stopped pounding through his body and he saw it as a window of opportunity to try anything.

Pat snatched back the cigarette. "So what's Pelican driving at?"

"The man said, That's the same thing everybody wants to know. It's supposed to be a mystery. I think it's just so you wonder what it's about."

"What makes the single so bad?"

"Pelican Driver / Are you gonna drive me? / Or should I be the driver? / Pelican Driver." AJ threw up his hands. "Dumb, dumb, dumb."

"Hmm. I'm not sure I get it."

AJ waved Pat's comment away, but couldn't wave away her cleavage even though he hadn't been looking there. In the occasional illumination provided by the light from passing vehicles, he could make out the two come-hither tips on her light cotton blouse. She didn't have on a bra. He swallowed. "There's nothing to get. It's a pointless song that won't go anywhere."

"Worse songs have become hits. At least your bird driver is making conversation."

AJ eyed Pat. He figured she had to be pushing thirty. But now she sounded thirteen.

Pat eyed him back. "You think I'm crazy? Just listen to the radio."

Pointed heels clicked behind them. They looked back. Antonia had stepped out of *Vogue* again. Tonight she wore a silky red body-clinger that would burn up any woman who didn't have the spirit of a vamp.

"Hot date?" AJ asked.

"I'm always hot." Antonia pouted. "My date can be a freezing Eskimo so long as he buys dinner."

Pat laughed. "That's the way, my girl!"

AJ got up and made room for Antonia to pass. He'd long suspected his sister augmented her salary from the furniture shop with her own peculiar brand of dabbling in the oldest profession, but he didn't intend to judge. Svelte yet exuding the innocence of a church choir teenager, Antonia simply rocked to high heaven. And AJ imagined many men would pay through hell to be with her. He couldn't bring himself to bother her. If it hadn't been for Antonia, they probably wouldn't have survived their parents' death in the air crash, and the abuse that followed at the hands of a so-called uncle.

"Are you coming back tonight?" he whispered as she passed by him.

"Why? Walk me to the road."

"You stopped asking why I don't get a girlfriend."

"You said you don't have the cash to date an Abuja babe."

"Well, yeah, it's that and …"

Blinding lights stabbed the night as a sleek Mercedes growled awake at the kerb. Antonia flashed AJ her best smile. "Anthony Junior, you want money, not so? Let's talk in the morning. And don't stare so much at Pat's boobs. She's too old for you."

AJ watched Antonia board the Merc. Why did she always think only the worst of him? He trudged back to Pat.

"Trouble?"

AJ shrugged. He felt certain Pat liked him, and though she hadn't that leggy look that he always sought in girls, her Coca-Cola bottle figure and that big ol' butt made him want to kick himself for keeping up the brotherly love charade for close to a year now. He considered telling her about the goings-on with his boss instead of saying anything that might make Antonia look bad.

"She paid for our room so that gives her the right to diss me," he said.

Pat gave him a hard look. "Sorry, man. You were telling me about Pelican's songs."

AJ understood. Pat may have asked but she didn't really want to know. Who really did in any case? "His second song is 'Find Work and Do'."

Pat blew smoke away from him. "You're joking."

"Find work and do / My brother don't be lazy / Sister you must get busy / Find work …"

"It's a lie," Pat said, cringing.

"Four lines for five minutes and I swear you haven't heard the worst of it. There's 'Come Out and Dance', 'Line Up Your Sorrows', 'Love is the Milk of Life', and …"

"Enough." Pat threw back her head and laughed hard. "Why are you producing if you hate the songs so much?"

"He's paid for every imaginable thing. Even things I didn't know existed, like pre-demo production tryouts."

"What the hell are those?"

AJ spread his palms. "I think my boss just wanted to get rid of him."

"But Pelican had money to burn."

AJ nodded.

"So, why you?" Pat stubbed out another cigarette.

AJ stared at the spot on the step where several cigarette butts now rested among the ashes. Pat saw him looking. She sighed, took off one of her slippers, and brushed the debris off the step.

"He said he heard I'm the best. Gave me a fifty thousand naira tip. Promised more if I give him a hit."

"Wow. So you're loaded. Buy a girl a drink now."

"I'm ready if you are."

Pat squeezed AJ's knee. "Save your money. Maybe you'll get your own room, eh? But how come he let you get off early?"

"He didn't. He tried telling me what to do, like some guys do in the studio. Then he had an accident with one of the big speakers."

She laughed. "An accident?"

AJ laughed too. "The speaker just happened to fall on his foot."

"Come on AJ, you can tell me."

AJ kept laughing. "I had nothing to do with it. He had to go have it bandaged or something. Said he'll be back but I guess he couldn't make it."

Pat shook her head. "You really hate that guy."

"I don't," AJ said, still amused.

More generators were running now and the neighbourhood had become an airport with several planes roaring to take off.

"Have you ever kissed a girl?" AJ asked.

Pat looked at him as if he'd been smoking something other than a cigarette. "Of course not. What sort of question is that?"

"Just a question."

"Have you ever kissed a boy?"

"No! But I've kissed a girl."

Pat sneered, got up and stretched. She bent backward and forward and AJ got a peek of her white underwear. He inhaled slowly and felt himself getting hard.

"Big party tonight," Pat said, brushing sand off the bum of her skirt as she turned to leave.

AJ swallowed. How he wanted to caress that ass. "Can I come?" he said.

Pat hesitated. "I'll have to ask Soso."

"So, so?"

"Soso." Pat giggled. "That's my friend's name."

AJ spoke to God often. Now he sent up some silent words. Please God, make this Soso person say it's okay.

God must have acceded, because an hour later AJ got into a taxi with Pat. They rolled into the grounds of Unicorn Palace, a mid-sized hotel in Wuse II, and Soso came downstairs to meet them. AJ noted Soso's lack of a butt as she led the way up to the party. "You've got lovely legs," he said.

Soso clucked. "Spare me the commentary."

"Who's the celebrant and what's he celebrating?"

Soso shot AJ a withering over-the-shoulder look. She eyed Pat. "Is he a journalist?"

Pat stepped ahead of AJ and clapped Soso on the shoulder. "Relax. AJ's cool. What's wrong with wanting to know what the party is for?"

"That's the kind of thing paparazzi always want to know. I don't know and I don't care." Soso grabbed Pat's waist. "Let's go. There's someone from the US you should meet."

AJ lived with it, consoling himself with a piercing stare at Pat's leather-clad bum as the girls clicked sexy high heels away from him. Whoever they were and whatever they were celebrating, they knew how to put together a party that popped. There were enough blazing babes in the place to give a monk a hard-on on sight.

But hold up: Pelican Driver, sandwiched between two burning bunnies, one heavily bandaged foot bossing a low corner table, had it going on, while Tweeshock's "Shame on Me" ruled the smoke-filled room.

AJ stepped up and shouted, "Yo Pelican! Now I see why you didn't come back."

Pelican's rough face smoothened into a smile. "AJ the champion rude boy. I thought you'd be locked up in that cage of yours until my hits are ready."

"Had to come out to play with my monkeys."

The girls laughed and AJ knew his night had begun.

"You have monkeys?" one of them said.

AJ jerked his thumbs at the empty spaces on either side of him. "George on the left. Georgina on the right. They're getting married when I win a Grammy."

Pelican laughed harder than the girls. AJ wanted to follow up with a line to get the girls' names, but Pelican stretched out a hand. "Help me up. You should meet the hostess."

For a man whose left foot sported a super-sized bandage, Pelican moved with relative ease. "Monica just returned from the States," he said as they stepped out into a wide corridor. "She's my backer, and today is supposed to be her birthday."

"Is it really?"

Pelican laughed.

AJ rolled his eyes. Not again.

Pelican opened a door marked OTTOMAN SPLENDOUR. They stepped into a suite from an *Arabian Nights* movie set. AJ checked for Ali Baba and his merry gang of forty. But it was Louis who stepped out of one of the doors wearing a satisfied smirk and a skinny girl on his arm.

"Choir boy," said Louis, seeing AJ. "So you party, eh?"

AJ had no answer, and Louis didn't wait for one.

Something tugged at AJ's heart. He eyed the retreating form of the skinny girl and wondered about the silly nature of jealousy.

"Monica should be here," Pelican said, trying the first door on the left. The man and the woman in the room didn't look like a Monica, and considering they were not having a little private chat, AJ wondered why they hadn't locked the door. The next door had been left unlocked too. AJ's eyes widened. A woman who looked like a darker Salma Hayek sat watching from a chair while a couple of babes locked lips and limbs on the bed. One clearly had no ass to speak of, but the other had enough to spare and had stuffed it into leather.

"Ah. I guess you'll meet Monica later." Pelican closed the door and beamed at AJ. "I have a room downstairs."

It sounded like an invitation, and AJ wondered why. Afterwards, whenever he thought about it, AJ would become sober. Somehow, he had already understood.

Pelican's room didn't belong to Ali Baba or any Ottoman sultan. Still, it could have been a page in a glossy magazine. AJ settled in front of the TV and picked up the remote. He flicked to Channel O.

"My producer, you've not had anything yet."

"If you've got malt, I'll take that."

"No beer, eh? You sober heads rule."

AJ had just taken a second sip from the bottle of Maltina when Pelican unzipped and popped himself out of his pants.

AJ gasped and backed away, spilling some of his drink. "I've never done this before."

"Don't worry," Pelican said, reaching out. "We all get to have first times."

AJ wanted to switch the topic. "Change the title of 'Find Work and Do'."

Pelican laughed. "You think it sounds bush, eh?"

"Well ..."

"That's the idea. Let it sound bush. I sing for the people. If I sound bush, the people will think they are better than me. If they're better than me, they will pity me; they will want to help me; they will want to *save* me. With their money."

AJ didn't believe he'd heard right. "That sounds–"

"Stupid?"

AJ nodded eagerly. "Don't you believe in the truth?"

Pelican kicked off his pants and guided AJ's hand to his swollen dick. "Truth? You don't understand people very much, do you? I studied sociology. What about you, my man?"

"Mass comm and music."

"Truth is what a majority of people at a certain place and time agree to believe. But people have a need to feel superior even when they're not. Give them that and they'll usually give you what you want, often without knowing it."

AJ shook his head. "That's hypocritical."

"And what's wrong with that?" Pelican's tone had no hint of humour. "Don't you know hypocrisy is just one of those things humans thrive on?" He pushed down gently on AJ's shoulders.

AJ got on his knees and fondled Pelican's throbbing penis. He shut his eyes. Damn what tomorrow would bring. He would ride this cloud until it turned to rain and poured him back to earth. He puckered his mouth and closed in.

Pelican moaned and spread his legs. "Is this why your boss calls you choir boy?"

AJ stopped sucking and looked up. "I *am* in the choir."

"Then sing me something champion, choir boy."

AJ resumed sucking. He sucked as if the outcome would be something incredibly worthwhile, like liquid gold and not mere sperm. Pelican moaned louder and shook.

Suddenly, he pushed AJ away. "Stop, stop," he panted. "I don't want to come yet. Take off your clothes."

AJ sat on the floor and began to undress. He looked up at the TV and saw Tweeshock's video playing. His face lit up.

"I came back to the studio, you know," Pelican said, chugging red wine straight from the bottle. "I saw you and your boss."

AJ got up and turned away. He tried to pull off his jeans but they resisted. He looked down and realised he'd stepped on them. He tried to hop off, tripped and fell. From the ground, he saw his scene on the TV. He didn't know what to think and suddenly didn't care.

Pelican helped him up. "It's okay, champion man. Don't break your bones. We all have our little secrets. Just remember to keep people thinking they're smarter than you or that you're no different from them."

At last, AJ got the jeans off and shrugged out of his shirt.

Pelican smiled comically. "You know you look like a girl?"

AJ sighed. Even though Pelican had that rugged look many bullies he'd known tended to have, he hadn't figured the guy that way. "Are you going to tease me about it?"

Pelican raised his hands in mock surrender. "I'm sorry. So they did that to you, too. I fought it all the time."

AJ frowned. "But you've got muscles."

"Seven years of gym work, man."

"Wow!"

"It's like the song, You made you more like me / So you'd be more like we / Same as chips in a diner / Now we're all Made in China / Shame on me / Shame on you / Shame on us!"

"You like Tweeshock! Cool." Suddenly AJ noticed Pelican's watch. "A Swatch. V cool."

"Tweeshock is okay." Pelican snapped off the watch and strapped it on AJ's thin wrist. "I like you."

Pelican settled on the bed and stretched out a hand. AJ took the hand and allowed himself to be pulled down.

Afterwards, he thought how it started out painfully, and then how his cloud of happiness grew into a comet of pleasure hurtling through the universe with him in a blissful trance. He couldn't believe the sensation. He'd never imagined anything could feel so intensely pleasurable. Had he been seduced? It would be an ugly lie to make that claim. He couldn't claim drunkenness. He'd had no access to hard drugs, so that was out too. It took a hand on his thigh. A certain look. And he went willingly into the embrace.

AJ moaned louder than Pelican. Then he tried keeping quiet. Finally, his emotions riding a riff, he broke into a shaky call and response solo.

"Pelican Driver,
Pelican Driver,
Are you gonna drive me?
Are you gonna drive me?
Or should I be the driver?
Should I be the driver?
Mister Pelican Driver,
Pelican Driver …"

Pelican's sweaty face was contorted beyond recognition. He stopped moving. "I like the way you sing it," he said, his voice husky and uneven. "That's how I'm going to sing it. That's how. That's how …" He began moving again, and though AJ had since shut his eyes, he knew Pelican's face looked like a man in tears. And so did his.

Afterwards, Pelican held out a new condom. "Your turn."

AJ tried to slip it on. He felt his body defy the AC with cold sweat. "I think the condom has expired."

Pelican frowned. "Seems to me you're the one who has expired." He stretched out sinewy arms. "That's okay. We all can't be top dog."

AJ ignored him, flung off the condom and began working himself. He didn't look much different from a plumber trying to jerk out a stubborn piece of piping.

Pelican smiled at the instant moderate result. "So you jump without a parachute?" He moved closer and began to help. "Dangerous, man. That is champion dangerous."

"All that live must die," AJ recited, ever more frantic in his tugging. He allowed himself to rest against Pelican's firm body.

"I see you know your Shakespeare."

"What Shakespeare?" AJ gasped. "It's in the Bi ... Bible."

"Wrong my man. Champion wrong. It's in *Hamlet* by William Shakespeare. Where in the Bible is yours?"

AJ's eyes glazed over as his hips bucked. Then he stretched out exhaustedly on the bed. "I don't know," he whispered. "And I don't care …" And thereafter in his memory, everything fell into three categories – before, during and after Pelican Night.

After the surprises of Pelican Night, AJ got out of the taxi first but waited for Pat to walk in front of him. He followed behind, resisting the urge to laugh at her hopping walk, which came from having lost one leg of her high heels.

Their neighbourhood still buzzed with the noise of electricity generating sets. Pat settled her ass slowly and seductively on her favourite step. She set down her bag, pulled out a wad of crisp dollar notes and began to count them.

"That's a lot of cash," AJ said, squeezing himself down next to her.

Pat lit a cigarette, inhaled and let out smoke. It hung in front of them in the early dawn cold. "Someone I met at the party wants me to do something for her. She didn't have naira so she gave me this."

"Looks like you've freed up all your tomorrows."

"What are you talking about?"

"Line up your sorrows / Let's stump on them all night / All of us with all our might / We can free up our tomorrows."

"If you sing any more Pelican drivel ..." Pat picked up the remaining leg of her shoe. "You two seemed to have gotten on very well."

AJ shrugged. "I've got to produce his album. It doesn't hurt to get along with him."

"So you still think he's a clown?"

AJ turned up his palms. "I read an opinion poll once where more than forty-five per cent of the respondents said they thought Tom Cruise is a big joke."

Pat threw back her head and let herself enjoy it. "Something strange happened tonight," she said when she stopped laughing.

"You mean other than losing your shoe?"

"I did something I've never done before."

"What?"

"It's funny because you asked me earlier."

AJ gave Pat a quizzing look as if he had no clue. "What are you talking about?"

Pat swallowed. "I kissed a girl."

"Oh."

"I mean, that's all I did but ... I feel weird."

AJ smiled and laid his arm across Pat's shoulders. "We all get to have first times."

The lights came on. A bulb hanging overhead made them both shield their eyes with their hands. Pat exhaled and looked AJ in the eye. "Are we going to sit here and talk till the sun comes up?"

AJ checked his Swatch. "It's almost four a.m." It seemed there were no secrets left. But he knew they'd both held back at least one thing each. Who knew how many things those ones subdivided into?

"Are you working today?" Pat said.

"No. Won't miss choir practice though. I'm singing a solo."

Pat led AJ by the hand into her room. She turned on a blue bulb and went to the bed.

AJ stood back. "I should tell you something."

"Are you gay?"

"No! God forbid!"

"I heard things about your Pelican at the party."

"Whatever you heard are lies. He's going to be huge. People are jealous."

"So what is it you want to tell me?"

AJ had wanted to tell her he'd kissed a boy. "I have condom-related erection loss."

Pat smiled and tugged at his jeans. "You see a condom and the little guy goes down?"

"Something like that."

"So you never use one?"

AJ shrugged. "I've avoided penetrative sex since I did the HIV test last year."

"Well, I should tell you something too."

"You're not a lesbian, are you?"

"No! Is that because I told you I kissed Soso?"

"Come on, Pat. You know I'm not like that."

Pat relaxed her hold on AJ's jeans. "I had syphilis some months ago."

"So? You took care of it, didn't you?"

Pat rolled her eyes. "Of course. But I've been scared to do an HIV test since then."

AJ nodded and pulled her close. "Even if you're positive, I don't believe your body will give anything bad to mine."

Pat punched him playfully on the chest. "You're crazy. You know that? Well, 'According to your faith be it unto you'."

AJ laughed. "Another fake Bible quote? I think you failed BK too."

"Who says it's fake? I can show you the–"

AJ's lips closed on hers.

Later on, Pat sang, "Pelican Driver, are you gonna drive me?"

AJ gave her a sharp look. "*You* are now singing Pelican's song?"

Pat trailed a finger on his smooth chest. "There's something about that one. Like it's a riddle, a secret code he's sending. I wish I could get it."

AJ exhaled slowly. "I've told you there's nothing to get. The song is meaningless. That guy is daft."

Pat stared at AJ. "You know you're a little snake?" She rolled away from him, studying him as if he were something freakish. Suddenly, she giggled.

AJ turned and faced her. "What?"

"You've got a girl's body."

"Tell me about it. I'm thinking of joining a gym."

"Don't. You're perfect like this. I like the way your body feels like a girl's. Plus you've got that something extra down there." Pat paused. Then she said, "You should have been the girl and Antonia the boy."

AJ shrugged. When they were growing up, he'd heard that a lot. For a long time, he took it as an insult. Now he'd learned to let it be. People saw what they wanted to see. And when Antonia saw the Tweeshock video scene, she could deal with it anyhow she liked. If Pat saw it, he'd tell her he'd kissed a boy, same way she'd kissed a girl: they were only acting in a video, nothing else happened, so help him God.

Pat tapped him. “Soso likes you.”

AJ’s brows went up. “It didn’t seem that way to me.”

“She’s that way. If she fancies you, she hides it by being nasty to you.”

AJ shook his head. “We did that in primary school.”

“Well, she’s still doing it. Many people still do it. She asked me if you and I were sleeping together and I swore we’re practically cousins.”

AJ chuckled and Pat pinched him. He seized her pinching hand and grabbed her butt. “There’s this popular saying in my home town: You keep saying he’s your cousin until we see your tummy shooting out. Now ‘cousin,’ come here.”

POISONED GRIEF

EMIL RORKE

With acknowledgements and gratitude to
HERMAN CHARLES BOSMAN – 30 JULY 2008

If you were to visit Pieter and Johanna Cornelius, you would not believe that the gaunt, taciturn woman in the kitchen was once vivacious, with sparkling blue eyes and a loud, happy laugh. Or that this kitchen, in which now only the ticking of the kitchen clock accompanied her impatient clattering, had been a place where women from the district met often to cook, joke and gossip, all to the accompaniment of the merry laugh and sparkling eyes of Johanna Cornelius.

You would not believe that the husk of a husband at her table, with his quivering mouth and dead eyes, was once a robust man, tall and proud, whose popularity stretched across the Marico, and whose company and advice were widely sought. He had been a man slow to take offence and quick to help, a generous pillar. Where once was strength was now feeble grief.

Also, you would not know that their daughter, Hettie, the laughing, dancing apple of her parents' eyes, had run away to Johannesburg with an English insurance salesman. Vague rumours of her godless life reached her parents irregularly, but never, in all the years since she had left, had she returned to see them.

The shadows of neither Pieter Cornelius, nor his wife, Johanna, had darkened the threshold of the church since their son died. At first,

Dominee Boonzaier and one or two ouderlinge had called shamefacedly, but, being met by silence and voiceless grief, had visited more intermittently. Finally, they stopped calling altogether.

Johanna Cornelius had been the centre of activity at the church bazaars, the leader of a happy band of women who had twisted and fried innumerable koeksisters and flipped countless pancakes. Now, the church bazaars produced floury pancakes and bitter, rock hard koeksisters from a group of dour women led by the listless wife of Ouderling Van Niekerk. Dominee Boonzaier had been heard to say that if the Lord could one day soften sister Van Niekerk's koeksisters, it would be a sign that he could soften even the heart of Johan Kriek, the district's obdurately drunken cattle thief.

Pieter Cornelius had been at the head of the men who had worked on the church building: painting, propping up the porch and repairing the roof. He had prevented a near tragedy when Dominee Boonzaier might have mounted the steps to a pulpit that had been eaten rotten by white ants. Later, Ouderling Van Niekerk, his mouth loosened by a surfeit of peach brandy at a wedding, had said that if only Pieter Cornelius had not fixed the pulpit, the subsequent collapse would have spared the church council the embarrassing job of telling Dominee Boonzaier that he was getting so fat that one day neither he nor the rich man would pass through the eye of a needle.

Work around the church was done now by a sullen Englishman and his sullen son. During a heavy rainstorm, when a stubborn drip of water above the pulpit had driven Dominee Boonzaier to say the closing prayer from the floor beside the pulpit, he had beseeched the Lord to make the windows of heaven as open to English sinners as the Englishman had made the roof open to the rain.

The shadows of Pieter and Johanna Cornelius had never again passed over the church threshold, and it was also as though the shadow of their tragedy would never leave the church, or its people.

You would not have known why, nor how, but I know. These are my people and I tell their stories. The art of telling my stories lies in saying the right things the right way, but sometimes, and sometimes more importantly, it lies in finding ways to say the things that are never said. It doesn't help, for instance, to say that the godless cattle thief Johan Kriek had lain with the daughter of the Tswana chief who bought his stolen cattle. It is better to say that now, when he comes to town, people see that Johan Kriek's Tswana trek boy has eyes that are uncannily blue, like those of his master, and a nose much alike, except that Johan Kriek's nose is brick red and covered with a stitchwork of blue veins.

Human lives and stories are like that. They consist as much in what can be told as in what cannot. Some things that are done cannot be talked about, much like Johan Kriek's lying with the daughter of the Tswana chief. You can talk about some things that happen, such as Dominee Boonzaier refusing to perform the funeral ceremony for Joey, the son of Pieter and Johanna Cornelius, but you cannot say why. You can say that the English priest finally buried the boy, he with his fluttery fingers and watery blue eyes, trying to talk Afrikaans and mangling the words of committal before the grieving relatives. You can say that people grieve, as Pieter and Johanna Cornelius did, but neither you nor they can talk about what other grief they have, beyond the grief of loss brought about by death. It is the unspoken, undisclosed grief that is the worst to see.

Mothers' hearts are soft towards their sons, and there are fathers whose hearts are also soft towards their sons. Soft in pride and in love, and with the hope that, one day, their sons may be as they are. The hearts of the young are soft, too, and become silly with love, and sometimes it is hard to tell where this soft, silly love may lead. Sometimes indiscriminately, and more than likely unwisely, young love may be claimed where it is found, and the warmth of a lover's embrace may be just what is needed to assuage the anxieties of life.

There was a time when the Lord smiled on this corner of the Marico. The rains came at the right time, and in the right amount. The sun, when it was hot, was not too hot, and the nights were not too cold. The crops were high, and the cattle fat. At the farm of Pieter and Johanna Cornelius and their twin children, Hettie and Joey, it was as though the laughter would never cease, nor the happiness ever be too much.

Their neighbour was Andries du Toit, a mordant man of shadowed countenance and dark moods, who seemed to shun God's sunlight. He and his wife, Trixie, and their son, Andreas, were seldom seen, either separately or as a family. At *Nachtmaal* they kept to themselves. When they went to the store and the post office, there was no conversation. Andries du Toit had that effect: he could stop a greeting dead in its tracks, much as a point three-oh-three bullet could stop a kudu bull. There was talk that Trixie du Toit wore a veil as much for modesty in church as to hide the bruises on her cheeks, and that Andreas du Toit walked, and sometimes sat, as though his body were bruised and sore.

Andries du Toit's farm was like him – unwelcoming and yielding of little. Its lands were rocky, and its cattle thin. It was as though the joylessness of the man had possessed the land, preventing God from visiting on his farm what He had bestowed on his neighbours. When Du Toit owned it, it had been called Opportunity Farm, but after Andreas's funeral, conducted also by the fluttery-fingered English priest, the Du Toits deserted the farm and the bank repossessed it. Later tenants of the farm fared no better, and the land was repossessed by the bank several times and became known as Repossession Farm.

There were skelms at the bank, said Dominee Boonzaier, who were very quick to advance money to honest men to buy scraggly, useless land, and the same skelms were quicker at taking back the land plus most of everything else the honest men had. Hell, said Dominee Boonzaier, would have so many skelms from the bank that there wouldn't be room for the Tswana and the English, and the godless people in Johannesburg.

It seemed as though Andries du Toit's shadow had stricken the land forever, much as the shadow of Pieter and Johanna Cornelius had stricken the church.

One Saturday, on a beautiful spring afternoon, an afternoon that can be had only in the Marico when the Lord has shone the light of his countenance on the district, the Cornelius family were in the kitchen, eating lunch together. Outside, in the yard, the dogs started barking and Pieter sent his son, Joey, to see what had alarmed them. Joey returned, with a hesitant Andreas du Toit behind him.

Andreas stood uncertainly on the kitchen threshold, holding his hat in his hands, curling and unfurling the brim with nervous fingers. He cleared his throat and said that his father had sent him with the message that some of his cattle had disappeared, and to ask whether Pieter Cornelius knew if the cattle thief, Johan Kriek, had been seen nearby.

Pieter Cornelius was startled to see Andreas du Toit, to whom he had never in his life spoken. He was about to say that Johan Kriek was too much of a clever thief to be interested in the Du Toits' scrawny cattle, but he checked himself, and instead asked the young man to join his family at their meal.

Andreas sat with the family for their abundant midday meal. The abundance was not confined to the food – it infused also the chatter and laughter of the family. The young visitor was clearly uncomfortable at first. He fiddled with the cutlery, spilt his food when he ate, never raised his eyes from the tablecloth, and answered in shy monosyllables when spoken to. Later, though, he thawed, and once, when Pieter Cornelius joked with him, he smiled. It could be seen that he had a strong, beautiful smile that lit his face and his eyes, and showed his even, white teeth.

Emboldened by Andreas's responses, Joey and Hettie continued to draw him out, and near the end of the meal he was almost as they were. Hettie suggested that they go outside, to the dam, after the meal. The young men and Hettie helped Johanna clear the table and tidy the kitchen, and then trooped to the dam. From the kitchen window, Pieter and Johanna watched the young people talking and laughing. A lump came to Pieter's throat as he watched them, and he thought how fine Hettie and Andreas looked together, she with her blonde hair and blue eyes, he with his dark hair and eyes, and the change in his face as his smile obliterated the seriousness.

In the late afternoon, Andreas came to the kitchen to bid farewell to Pieter and Johanna, and to thank them for their hospitality. Impressed by his manners, they invited him back, and were sure to tell him that they had not seen hide nor hair of the cattle thief Johan Kriek.

The first few Saturdays that Andreas returned, he came with a message or request from his father. It was clear that they were spurious, fictions to give him an excuse to visit. Pieter and Johanna were happy: Andreas was a pleasant young man and Hettie bloomed at his visits. Only Joey seemed a little downcast, but the parents ascribed his demeanour to jealousy over Andreas's closeness with Hettie.

One Saturday there was a sudden, violent thunderstorm, and Andreas could not walk home in the lightning and the rain. When the storm ended it was too late for him to walk home. Pieter had a stone shed at the end of his barn in which he kept seeds and farm tools. It was warm and dry, and Joey helped Andreas make a bed for himself in the shed, and Andreas spent the night there.

That was the first of many Saturday nights that Andreas spent at the Cornelius farm. It was also the time when Hettie's parents felt hope for their daughter's heart, but sadness also, because the bringer of this hope came from the dark neighbouring farm. But neither parent could deny the benign influence of Andreas, even on Joey, whose mood had lifted, and who was as animated as Hettie when Andreas was there.

Pieter and Johanna felt some guilt, for they were sure that there were repercussions for Andreas for his absences from his father's farm, but they never raised the matter. They came to believe that Andreas's visits would not have continued had his father become too harsh, and they delighted in the love of their family that was extended to the lonely young man. Their children's happiness and the benign weather seemed to promise an endless bounty to Pieter and Johanna.

The English doctor, sent from Zeerust, said that it was the fumes from the insecticide and fertiliser in the barn that were fatal. He made a note of all the chemicals that Pieter Cornelius kept there, and wrote a long report in English, which was read at the inquest. He explained how various chemicals could set alight and give off poisonous fumes when they were heated above a certain temperature, and others, while not setting alight, could heat up and give off mortally toxic gases. The report was difficult to follow, but it was clear about one thing: that nobody would have survived the poisonous fumes.

That fateful night, Hettie was the first in the house to see that the barn was alight. She ran to her brother's room to get him to warn Andreas, who was sleeping in the stone shed, but Joey's bed was empty. She woke her parents, and the three ran outside. They hoped to find Joey out there, but could see nothing in the dark and the smoke from the fire. The noise of the burning was so loud that their voices, when they called for Joey and Andreas, were lost in the roar of the fire.

The family stopped calling, and stood together, watching in awe the destruction of their barn, wondering in terror what might have happened to Joey. Johanna started weeping, and her daughter Hettie held her, then broke down herself.

Pieter Cornelius tried desperately in the dark to lead water from the dam to the fire. The trickle vaporised when it hit the heat, but Pieter left the water running, giving no thought to the needs of the cattle for water the next day. He rejoined his wife and daughter, and held them, finally himself breaking into sobs.

A sudden, short rainfall mercifully extinguished the blaze in the early hours of the morning, but it was too dark, and the smouldering remains too hot, for anyone to go into the barn.

In the near light of dawn the next morning, the barn had cooled sufficiently for Pieter to walk gingerly into the ruins. He had spent the remainder of the night looking around in the dark to see if perhaps Joey and Andreas were unconscious in the veld. His search had been in vain, and now he looked about with apprehension to see whether, in the dawn light, he might find a burned body. But he found none.

The stone shed had remained intact, and its door, miraculously, had been only half burned. With dread Pieter pushed open the door and saw the body of the young man, Andreas du Toit, naked on his makeshift bed. And beside him, with their limbs intertwined and his head on the bosom of Andreas was the body of his son, Joey. Also naked.

THE BATH

WAMUWI MBAO

I run a bath for myself and for your memory in my head, two weeks after.

Your father drove thirty kilometres yesterday, just to say he was sorry. He found me cleaning the house. "You're messy for girls," he said. I've never been good at that sort of thing. We never lived like they did in those movies: white thick-pile carpets, low luxurious bed, box lampshades. Ours was not a world Tom Ford would be interested in. We spilt pasta on the floor and our couches were over-stuffed. Your T-shirts said things like FYI – I HIT LIKE A BOY. I've held on to that one, some small trace of you.

I stop up the door with towels: I think that's how it is done. I commit myself to the water, first one foot, then the other. I read the label on the luminous can: instructions for cleaning one's carburettor. I spray until the fumes fill the bathroom and the can emits no more of its cloying varnish-sweet contents. I slip lower into the hot water. I'm reading your journal. Maybe that's not the best thing to be doing: I don't want it to be ruined.

I kissed you on the mouth three days after we met. You said it was a complication you could do without, and then you smiled. *Saturday with Olivia – nice.* ☺: the moment is recorded in your journal. We held hands on Lerato's couch in the aftermath of a Kirstenbosch Gardens concert. You were wearing your brother's hat. I can't explain the state I was in. I fell asleep on your shoulder. Though we have sparred since then, though we have had our silences, that moment is one I return to.

I'm falling into the insistent hypnotism of soothing water and noxious solvent.

You ran down Long Street on your first weekend back, and you made me follow you. I couldn't keep up. We met your friends from university, the ones whose names I don't remember. *Thabiso and Lorcia make a cute couple.* Did I meet them? Is it all over now? We snuck into your parents' house at three a.m., raided the fridge. I think about that night every time I can't sleep. That shouldn't be a problem anymore. Change is absolute.

The water level is higher than I usually like it.

One Sunday you read my writing. "If you don't show anything, you can write whatever you like," I reassured you. You told me you were scared of what your father would say if he found out. He knows now, and I think he knew when we visited them that weekend. Your mother came by the day before yesterday, made soup. It was her way of understanding, you once said. She looks like you, when nobody's watching her.

It's two a.m. and the monotony of the bath begins to get to me. I think of nothing. My head doesn't even have the decency to spin from these supposedly toxic fumes. "Chemical solvents," you would have said, "are ill-suited to the task of snuffing out a human life." Overcome by the shame of it all, I wrap myself in a towel and place your journal on the pile of laundry I've been folding.

You never folded the laundry. You alphabetised the books. We compromised on the battle of music, but our books still jostle for space on the bookshelf, your classics alongside my crime.

You said that being black was a state of mind. I said I didn't care what colour you were. We didn't know what to call ourselves, so you'd make up something new every time someone asked. I wonder what you told people when I wasn't there. You had a thousand faces I'll never know.

We travelled downtown once, looking for old records to stick on our wall. I hoped you'd take my hand when those boys were making eyes at you. You told me that we were not molecules, that we didn't need observers to watch us clank together.

The way you looked at me made my eyes hurt. Your face when you were stirring pancake batter, how you looked unbeatable at the top of the slide in the park. You were a little short for your age. People always commented on that. You took more risks because of it.

I knew, even before trying, that my attempt would fail. I can't follow you, but there's a joyous recklessness in trying.

You worried about your father. He worried about you. "He needs to eat less salt," you said. "She needs to like boys," he said. You would not be trapped by them, you vowed.

We shared the same ideal of the world's beauty, could embrace the simplicity of hummus on toast and a shiny colander. "What will we do for money?" I asked. "I'll write the Great South African Novel," you said, "and you'll wear long dresses and braid my hair."

You made my heart skip a beat. Yours skipped far too many when it shouldn't have. Like that Thursday when you grew cold and I almost crashed, driving too fast to the hospital. A heart's a funny thing. An irregular thing. I used to listen to the weird rhythm of yours. I could feel the hard outline of your pacemaker beneath your skin, below your breast. Two days in a hospital bed, and your heart decided to be still.

You said you wanted to live again, when I last dreamed of you. That was last weekend. I put your things in boxes, kept what I thought I could, gave to your parents what I thought they would want. I drove by the next day, and the day after that, in case they threw your things out. I strummed your guitar. The last thing you played for me was "Saudade". I asked you what that song meant. You called it a remembrance of things past.

Sometimes you yearned for the quiet life. You yearned to be skinnier. "Nobody likes a fatty," you said. I protested, spoke about culture, and I squeezed your waist, and you laughed. You were into plain sailing, and saying what you meant. You were for the workers, for the revolution, whenever that came. "Stay irresponsible," you once told me. You thought great universal thoughts. I tried to keep up. That book is closed now, I guess. Time to begin another one.

You purposely lost us once, just to prove that it could be done. I don't know if I can capture those moments again. In their place is a layer of loneliness which pushes down on me. It may suffocate me if I'm not careful. Maybe that's good. If I give myself over to despair, then I won't have to venture out in the sunshine like the world hasn't noticed: the leaves, the flowers.

I emptied a tub of frozen yoghurt into the sink last night. It was the last thing you ate before time stopped. Time stops when your heart stops beating. The doctor said that you didn't suffer. Thank death for that small mercy. No joy in observing that terrible monster. You joked about the ignominy of slipping in the bathtub. My feet were flat, like a hobbit's feet, you said. We pressed our feet together, yours brown, mine pale. We waltzed around the flat then, high on cheap champagne and the joy of being close.

I stub my toe when I return the towel to the rack. No matter. It reminds me, I think, that I am alive.

CHAPTER THIRTEEN

K. SELLO DUIKER

My mind races with a million things. From where I'm sitting I can see everything. I can hear everything. All of it, the music, the patting of feet as people run, the dogs barking, cars rushing. I can hear it all, even my own heartbeat in my ear. And it all makes sense. Not good sense or bad sense, just sense. I scratch my balls and think about all the money Joyce stole from me. She's a bitch, a fucking cunt. It was a lot of money.

The moffies walk by. One of them looks at me but I pay no attention to him. I just look out at the sea. Another sits beside me and opens his legs. A big banana is between his legs.

"I like your pants," he says and brushes his shoulder against mine.

"You're full of kak," I hear myself saying.

He closes his legs but still sits beside me.

"What do you want?"

"You can sleep over if you want. You look clean."

I think about it and say nothing.

"Okay, I'll cook for you."

"Does your wife know you do this?"

"No. She's away on holiday," he says a little nervous.

"Well, take off your ring. I don't want to see it," I almost shout at him.

"Done," he says and pulls it off.

"Why do you wear it?"

"Because I'm married."

"No. I mean …"

"Oh, I don't know. Habit, I guess. Also I don't want to lose it."

You've lost your mind, I say to myself.

"You have kids?"

"Look, I don't want to talk about my family. Are you coming or not?"

I look at him concealing his big banana and smile.

"I'm just waiting for the sun to go down."

We sit on the bench and say nothing as the sun gently touches the water. I always imagine that steam will go into the air when this happens but it never does. The sun just goes quietly into the water and disappears. The clouds become red with fire. On the other side of the sky I can see the colour of bruises.

"We better go," he says, "it's getting late."

You mean you're worried that someone might see you, I say to myself.

"I'll do it for fifty," I say as I get up.

"A bed, food and fifty. You drive a hard bargain," he says.

"Have you ever slept out here?" I say and look into his eyes.

He says nothing and walks in front. White people are full of *kak*, I say to myself.

We walk slowly as I don't have my crutch. Joyce, that bitch, I think.

"What happened to your leg?"

"I fell and broke it."

"What, your leg?"

"No, this part here," I say and point to my ankle.

"Is it sore?"

"Not really. I'll have it off in a couple of weeks. This thing I mean."

"I know."

We go to his car first. He takes out two boxes and a plastic bag, the type dustbin people use. He gives me the plastic bag to hold. We go to a nice block of flats near Sunset Beach. It's the best block I've ever been to. Outside there's a guard. "Hi, Alfred," he greets him as he lets me inside. When he's not looking Alfred gives me the evil eye. I stick out my tongue between my gap and cross my eyes.

"You better park your car in the garage, Mr Lebowitz, we've had some burglaries outside the building," he says in a deep grownup voice.

"Fine, Alfred," he says as we get into the lift. We go up many floors, almost reaching the top floor. As we get out I look out of a row of large windows and see the sea.

"You live here?" I say.

He smiles and brushes my bum. We go into his flat. Almost everything is white. Strangely I feel calm. He takes the plastic bag and offers me a seat. His manners are sickening. They are perfect and make you feel a little strange, like you're a dog with fleas. And he has to be careful around you. I ignore his manners and make myself comfortable. I sit on a white leather sofa. It's so soft I could fall asleep on it. He does something in the other room. I can hear cupboards opening and closing. I get bored and my eyes stray to the big TV. I'm shocked to see myself on the screen. I move closer and the image of myself moves closer as I move closer to the screen. I sit back and the image also sits back. For a while I just stare at myself stupidly. White people are evil, I say, and turn off the TV. I sit there and wait for him but I can't stop wondering about that TV. Where are the cameras? I wonder, and I look around the room. I can't see any cameras, only a neat room with lots of beautiful things. This guy is sick. He's going to film the whole thing.

"I thought we'd take a shower first," he says when he comes in.

"You mean you're horny."

"Are you always this direct?"

"Do you want to fuck me?"

"Good God," he says and walks over to the piano where there are pictures of his family. He turns them all over as if they will see and hear everything.

"Look, if you're going to be like that you can get out now. I've tried being nice to you."

"Sorry," I say and grind my teeth.

"Just don't do it again."

"Look, that's how it is. They all speak to me like that."

"Well, I'm not them."

"Don't worry, I won't ask you your name."

"Good."

"Just relax, okay. I also want to have some fun," I lie and put on a smile.

"Well, I'm tense now," he says and goes to the other room.

"Can I put on the TV?" I ask.

"It's broken," he says, and returns with a glass of wine.

"Is it alright if I take off my T-shirt? It's a little hot."

"Ja, sure, but I can put on the air-conditioning."

"Don't worry. I'll be fine," I say and take off my T-shirt.

"You've got the most incredible blue eyes for a …"

"Darkie," I smile.

"Yes," he says awkwardly. "Are they real?"

That is the strangest question I've ever heard.

"What do you mean?" I ask and sit closer next to him.

"I mean, are they contact lenses?"

"What?"

"Never mind. I guess they're real."

He puts down his glass on the table. I put my hand on his crotch and rub it. He opens his pants and his dick pops out. I stroke it gently.

"You like that, don't you?" I say while I rub it.

I know how to please a man. I know these bastards. I've done this a thousand times. They all like it if you play with the part between their balls and asshole. And you must not pull too hard on the dick. It's better if you play with the dick as close as possible to the tummy, otherwise they say it's sore or it starts flopping. And the older they get the more it doesn't stand up against their tummy. One guy's dick was still down but it was hard. And he wasn't that old. I think he had a problem with his *piel*. Poor bastard. Imagine having a broken *piel*.

Another thing is I never ask them how that feels. They hate that question. I think it reminds them of their boyfriends or their wives or whoever it is they are cheating on. The other thing is if you ask you get strange requests. I don't want to think about some of the things I've had to do to these bastards. No thank you.

"Let's go to the bathroom."

"Wait. I have a problem with my leg. I can't shower."

"Then you'll bath and I'll shower."

We go to the bathroom. It has white tiles on the floor that show off your reflection. And there is a large mirror on one wall. You can see your whole body when you get naked. And there are two toilet seats but one of them has little taps. It looks broken.

"I've never seen myself like this before," I say looking at the mirror.

"You mean naked?"

"No. I've seen myself naked before, just not on a mirror this big and with all this light."

"Oh," he says and runs a bath for me. I feel stupid for saying that.

"Are you hungry?"

"Not really," I lie and look at the white bath.

The taps are made of gold. Can you believe it, Blue? Gold. The fucking taps are made of gold. This guy must be loaded with baksheesh.

"Not too much," I say.

He closes the taps and gives me some soap and a towel. I get into the bath and hang my knee over the edge.

"Clever boy," he says and gets into the shower.

Fuck, I'm glad I washed at Gerald's. Imagine if he had to see my brown dirt.

We wash quickly and I clean out the bath with a sponge afterwards.

He gets out the shower, his banana dick bouncing everywhere. He reaches out and strokes my face. I shake his dick and say "Pleased to meet you," like white people do. He laughs a little and takes my hand.

We go to his room. There is a large window and a bed far away from the window. "Sit here," he says, and goes to the window to close the curtains. I bounce a little on his big bed. It's nice and hard.

"Is this your room?"

"No, it's the guest room," he says and puts on the light.

He spreads me on the wide bed and starts sucking my dick. That's never happened before. I start giggling.

"Sorry, I've never had this," I say.

He ignores me and carries on. After a while the pleasure turns into sadness.

"I'll do it to you," I say.

He turns over and lies on his back. I take his banana dick in my hand and start stroking it. He lets out a long sigh. I play with his balls and the part underneath his balls. When I put my mouth on his head he moans a little and closes his eyes. I don't think about anything else. I just suck and play with my tongue on his banana dick. He starts breathing funny like he's going to pass out. Then he grabs my wrist and a fountain of sperm pours out of his banana dick and lands on his chest. It's over when that happens.

They all lie back and don't want to be touched. All that I can hope for now is that he will keep his other end of the bargain.

"Just give me some time," he says.

"You mean you still want to go?"

"Who's paying here?"

"I was only asking," I say and play with his balls.

After a while his banana dick rises again.

"Lie back," he says, "I want to come all over you. Do you mind?"

"No. Just don't squirt on my face."

He starts playing with himself while he stands over me. They all seem to enjoy this. I guess it feels like pissing to them.

After a while, a long while actually, he comes all over my chest. "Thank you," he says, "I've been dying to do that all day."

"It's a little hot, isn't it?" he says and puts on the air-conditioning.

I go to the toilet to get my clothes.

"Don't bother with them," he says.

We walk around the house naked. I have the feeling people are watching me, or rather that a camera is following me. He walks around in his slippers. I follow him to the kitchen. He opens a large silver door and a cold breeze comes out. The shelves are stacked with food.

"What do you fancy? We can either have turkey on our sandwich or cheese."

"Turkey and cheese," I say.

He takes them both out and a cabbage. I watch him prepare the food. He's good with his hands.

"So what do you do?" I ask him. "If you don't mind."

"I'm an investment banker."

"But what do you do?"

"I work with lots of money."

"It must be a hard job," I say.

"It is."

"So you work here in Cape Town?"

"That's right."

Investment banker. He's probably the bastard who took my money, I say, thinking of Joyce.

"So is it hard for anyone to open a banking spot at your place?"

"You mean opening an account. I'm afraid I don't do that sort of work."

"Oh. So you're like the boss."

"Something like that. I have a lot of people working for me. But I know what you're talking about."

We sit at the table. He pours me some orange juice in a tall glass.

"This is strange," I tell him.

"What?"

"Walking and eating naked like this."

"You don't like it?"

"No, it just feels strange. But a good strange."

He chews with his mouth closed. As always I eat quickly.

"Had enough?" he asks, after I have finished four slices of bread.

"Yes."

I wanted to say thank you but it just wouldn't come out. We go to the other room with the big television. He puts on some music.

"You know what this is?"

"No, but I've heard it before."

"Classical music. Carl Orff, *Carmina Burana*. He's like your ... rap artists or whatever you listen to."

He sits on a chair for one and grabs some cigarettes from the table beside him.

"Can I have one?" I ask as he lights one.

He takes one out but he doesn't pull it all the way out of the pack. He offers me the one pointing at me. His manners are maddening. I can see him. He thinks about everything all the time.

We smoke in silence and listen to the music. The songs are long. But I like the music. It does something to your insides. It lets you relax.

"But this music is violent," I say after a while.

"It is, isn't it? *Carmina Burana* is not for the fainthearted. Listen to this part."

The strings reach fever pitch and people sing around beating drums.

"What is that instrument?"

"Violin."

"You like music, don't you?"

"Ssssh," he says, "listen."

I listen with him for about thirty minutes and fall asleep. He wakes me. He's already dressed.

"I just need to park the car in the garage downstairs. Don't get up to any mischief. Oh, and you can't leave the building without me. So just behave. I'll be back in a while," he says and leaves.

As soon as he leaves I put on the TV again. This time the TV shows the room we were doing it in. I go in there and look for the cameras but I can't find them. It starts feeling creepy walking around the house naked. Is this guy a pervert or something? I say as I put on my clothes. I walk around the rooms but only in the ones where the doors are open. In two of them the doors are locked. So this is how people who work in banks live. They are always being watched. I wouldn't want all his money if it meant I had to live like that. To always have people watching you is a curse. I turn off the TV.

I sit on the couch. I start to feel a little sad. No, I tell myself. I must be strong. I am strong. I get up and go to the kitchen. I drink from the tap, my mouth around its mouth. I drink lots till my stomach says enough. I feel better, I tell myself and go back to the couch. Why do you feel sad? I ask myself. Because my mother didn't love me. Gerald is cruel. That is the ugliest thing anyone has ever said to me. It is worse than having a bus crush you. I think of my mother and feel confused. No. She loved me, I tell myself. And I loved her, no matter what Gerald says. He's just like Allen. He wants to control me. I look around and realise that there are no stupid pigeons watching me, only hidden cameras. You're never completely on your own, I say. Only when you are born and when you die. Nobody cares when you die. They just want to know what you will leave them. I remember my father saying that about my grandfather after he died. I hope he left me that watch, he kept saying. He never did get it. The relatives came before we did and cleaned out my grandfather. I don't want to think about my family. But you have to, a little voice says inside me.

What's there to think about? My mother died. My father died. I hiked to Cape Town with Mandla, Vincent. And now I'm here. There's nothing much to say. There's nothing much to think about. I can't write. I can't phone my relatives. They don't care about me anyway. And I don't miss them. I don't miss them because they never gave me anything. And that's alright, at least they didn't give me bullshit like Cape Town grownups. I feel better when I say this. You see. Sea Point. I'm getting stronger.

He returns and finds me with my clothes on.

"I thought we'd have another go," he says.

I take off my clothes in the room. His banana dick bounces out of his pants again as he takes them off.

"Wait," he says and runs into the other room. He puts on the music, different music but still the same whining, stringy music.

"Vivaldi, *Four Seasons*. I've always wanted to do this."

He lies on top of me and just grinds his hips against mine.

"Why aren't you getting an erection?" he says.

I think of Toni Braxton and my dick rises.

"That's better," he says and carries on rubbing himself against me. "This time I want you to come with me."

"Ready when you are."

"Really? Just like that."

"It's true."

"Okay wait. I'll tell you."

He doesn't tell me. His eyes just start rolling into their whites and he grunts to the music.

"Oh heaven," he says as the music rises. "Are you coming too?"

"Yes," I say and nearly laugh at the funny look on his face.

Then he just falls on me and sighs.

"That was great. You killed me. I'm completely annihilated."

"It doesn't take much," I say.

"You and the music," he says and gets up to wipe himself. He throws the towel at me. Strange, he usually hands me things. We both put on our clothes and go to the music room. He sits on the chair and smokes alone.

"You like this music, don't you?"

He says nothing. He looks sad, a little angry or hurt. I can't tell. Grownups are hard to figure out.

"It's Winter," he says.

"What?"

"The music. It's called *Four Seasons* and now it's Winter."

I listen.

"Listen carefully. Can you see the trees without leaves?"

Trees. I know trees. I listen to the music. It is too much. I go into the other room and sit on the couch. This guy is trying to open me up. He thinks he's clever. Of course he's clever, he owns a bank. Him and Joyce are all from the same team. Don't forget that, I remind myself.

"I feel tired," I say when he comes back.

"I was going to play you this one song by Mussorgsky."

"I'm really tired," I say and put on puppy eyes.

"Okay, come," he says.

We go back to the room. He opens the bed.

"Will this pillow be enough? I can get you another one if you want."

"No, it's fine. Actually I like sleeping without one."

The street, I can hear him thinking, but his maddening manners prevent him from saying it.

"Where are you going to sleep?"

"I don't know. I might sleep in here. I don't know. Goodnight." He switches off the light and leaves the door open.

I get into bed but sleep doesn't come easily. I stare at the ceiling and try not to think much. Too much thinking is bad for you. Look at all the grownups I know. They're all fucked in the head. They should be smoking *zol*. And that poor bastard in there, he doesn't know whether to leave or to come. At least I have new pants and a new T-shirt. But I'll need a new jacket for the days when it gets cold. I know. I'll buy a jacket from the place in Long Street. I'm sure I can get something there. But I must be careful. I mustn't buy like a *moegoe*. I must buy a sensible jacket. Vincent said I must be the blackest person he knows. I still don't understand what he means by that. He said I must buy from *makwerekwere*. I can if I want to now; I don't have to think about Allen. And I don't think Gerald will mind. In fact I think Gerald wants me to do things for myself. I'm not going to ask him. I'm just going to buy it. That's right. No thank you, Gerald. I'm just going to buy it.

Now if only I could sleep. My neck hurts. I must sleep now. Tomorrow I'm going to get a new jacket. That's something to look forward to. And I don't have to look at Allen anymore or Joyce, that bitch. I hope she gets boils all over her pussy and that stupid white man who does ugly things in the dark with her. I hope his *piel* rots. They're both evil. But I'll miss Sea Point. I'll still come back when I can. I just won't go anywhere near them. I'll just stay on the beach road. And I'll buy a towel and maybe one day I can take a dip in that pool and buy myself an icecream like I always say I will. It's all going to be fine. I can take their bullshit. All of them. Even Gerald.

But I hope Vincent doesn't go. Why did Bafana say that? Was he also fucking with me? No, Bafana likes me. He wouldn't say that unless it was true. Vincent can't go. He's my connection. The only one I have in Cape Town. Without him I'll have no one. And everyone has a connection, even if it's just one person in the whole world. No, he can't go. I'll talk to him tomorrow. I think of Vincent as my eyes. He's older than me. He's seen more, done more. I don't think anything scares him anymore. Everything seems to make sense to him. Vincent, he's a grownup but not like the others. He doesn't bullshit. He just says it like it is. He just stays Vincent, Mandla; the guy I grew up with in Mshenguville. He's alright, Vincent. He always looks out for me. All the things he tells me, they help me. They help me become like him, a man, a grownup.

He changes the music. The saddest music I ever heard comes out. But it's a gentle sadness that doesn't take you all at once. It just goes by you but you feel it. It's a soft sadness. I look at the light coming through the room and wonder what he's doing. But I'm too tired to get up. I just listen to the music while I beg sleep to come.

I can hear the piano. The softest notes seem to fly. Rising and falling like a seagull flying. This guy is fucked, I say to myself. To listen to music like this you must be fucked. And he probably listens to it while his wife is there but she doesn't know what's going on in his head. That's fucked, I say, and listen to the notes rapidly playing before they disappear into quiet, slow notes. The music always ends gently. When the song ends I close my eyes and grab all the sleep I can get in this warm room.

LOWER MAIN

TO MOLEFE

My friend Madz and me are at Obz Café, a nothing little eatery on Lower Main Road. It's not my kind of kind of vibe, but Madz likes it. Back when we used to speak more frequently, before she ran off to the southern suburbs with her girlfriend TeeKay, she told me she liked it because it's usually occupied by foreign students roughing it at the backpackers lodge upstairs or artsy types from the indie theatre next door. She also liked how, like everything else on the street, it was laid back and unadorned.

We're sitting outside because Madz has recently started smoking. She's looking thin. Her sullen cheeks, spiky moulded afro and those eyes, rimmed by dark eyeliner, all make her look like a newly hatched raven. Her skin glistens like feathers slicked down by albumen. Still, she's as gorgeous as ever; her sculpted eyebrows, those dewdrop lips. I have to tear my eyes away.

Observatory's busier than it's been in a while. Spring's finally arrived, with the bustle of a date you thought had stood you up, and Lower Main's inhabitants have slunk out of their pits of self-effacement to turn the street, for a brief moment, into a kaleidoscope of freakishness. Two tourists, a man and a woman, appear to be out of place. They gawk at each person they see. How do I know they're tourists? I don't. But just look at them. He's wearing inappropriately short shorts, a floral print shirt and a camera around his neck.

She's wearing tan capris and a tight, sleeveless knitted sweater. The man stops to take pictures of *bergies* passed out with their mouths open outside the liquor store. If this were my first time on Lower Main, I'd be shocked to see someone taking pictures of homeless drunks. But it's not. So I'm not. As he snaps away, the woman tugs at his arm. It's not cautioning. It looks like she's urging him on.

I turn back to Madz to see her lick back the last of her beer, her salamander tongue flashing around the lip of the bottle.

"Uh, Madz? That's your second in ten minutes," I say.

"And?"

"You're drinking like you're on fire. You okay?"

"I'm fine, and don't mother me. You know I don't like that."

"I know," I say. "You just never used to smoke or drink ..."

Madz looks away from me and into the café.

I first met Madz when I responded to her ad for a buxom black woman to pose nude for sketches. It read just like that. WANTED: BUXOM BLACK WOMEN FOR NUDE SKETCHES. NATURAL HAIR ONLY. Full-figured women apparently make interesting subjects, and I'd made a sort of career doing that kind of thing. There was really nothing to it. Just step into a studio or a room in a bourgie house, and disrobe. It was usually for an art class for well-to-do, liberal housewives, bored with découpage and painting fruit. They weren't afraid to speak like I was a bowl of fruit. "How'd her butt get SO big?" one once asked. At a different class, another said, "I long for the courage to stop obsessing about my weight like she has." None of this ever bothered me and the money was good. Sometimes, I got lucky. I'd end up posing for a real artist.

I didn't pose for Madz. We got talking, and I just never got round to disrobing. We spoke like old friends, our conversation breaking into multiple strands, converging and breaking again. We spoke about her work. She was doing a series of portraits back then, all charcoal and pencil – nudes of disembodied bodies. Their pencil outline seemed unable to contain their charcoal filling. All their faces were detailed but smudged grotesquely. She said she was trying to capture truth, but it seemed to me too obscure a concept to understand. Not truth, but her trying to capture it. When it was all done, there was something about the portraits. Maybe the white spaces around the smudged black and white forms, or the forms themselves, but something seemed to be missing in an aching kind of a way. The portraits got her exhibition space at a few galleries. That's how she met TeeKay, an art programme dropout who'd used her trust fund to fashion herself as a gallery curator.

"Madz," I say. I reach for her hands across the table. "You know this comes from a place of love, right? You look in a bad way, friend."

She pulls her hands away and carries on staring into the café. I pick up my beer and suck it down. I wave to the waiter for two more. When Madz finally speaks, she confirms a rumour I've been hearing. TeeKay has broken up with her.

"Sorry," I say, "but I told you two people so different can't get on forever."

"Fuck, Dee," she says, turning to look me dead in the eye, "that's the nicest thing anyone's said to me in a while."

"I just mean you two never had that much in common."

"You've said this many, many times before."

A knowing silence descends. She's waiting for me to explain myself. I'm waiting for her to let me off the hook.

"I just never liked TeeKay for you," I say, blinking first.

"You've never liked anyone for me," she says.

She pops open a box of Stuyvies and pulls two out. One goes into her mouth and the other behind her ear. She looks back into the café and I steal a look at her long neck flexing, the muscles, tendons and bone shifting beneath the skin. It's all I can do to keep from reaching out.

It's true. I've never liked anyone for her. It's just that more than anyone I know, Madz doesn't like lying to herself. But sometimes, just to survive, you need to lie, or at least play pretend, every now and then. I got this about her, but not many people did. Not many would. TeeKay certainly didn't. She dismissed Madz as eccentric. She saw her as a project, a vintage store trinket she got for next to nothing and spruced up, just to prove to her friends that she could create.

Madz catches me staring. For the tiniest moment, it looks like she's about to say something. Instead, she looks over my shoulder. I turn around and look too.

The tourist couple are looking at posters of women with different hairdos outside Sheena's African Hair Parlour. They are pointing and speaking, and it seems quite an academic discussion. A debate, maybe. Perhaps she's curious if there exists any evolutionary consequence from women who dress up their hair in other women's hair? But he thinks, if anything, the only consequence is psychosocial. The sound of splashing behind them catches their attention – a dreadlocked redhead emptying water from a green hubbly into a storm drain. The man points his camera and starts snapping away.

I turn back to Madz. "Do you mind my asking what happened?" I say.

She's lit the cigarette and is holding it between her index finger and thumb. She tries to smile, but her smile crumbles to a grimace. "I stopped showering," she says.

"I've had days like that," I say, "days where I couldn't be bothered. But they never last."

"This wasn't like that. There was, I dunno, more to it." Madz shifts in her seat. She puts her cheek against the glass of the window.

"For how long, Madz?" I say.

"Who knows? I lost track of time. It all became the same with no signal that a new day's started. I skipped a couple of showers in the beginning. I was distracted, feeling antsy. But when TeeKay didn't tell me I stink, I skipped another day to see what she'd say."

"Did she even notice?"

"If TeeKay did notice," she says, "she didn't say anything."

I wait for her to go on. She cups her hand under her chin and bites her pinkie nail. She stares at the smoke rising from her ciggie, sitting in the ashtray between us.

"I could feel the grit building up on my skin, you know? I'd rub my arm and there'd be little rice-shaped kernels," she says. She picks up the ciggie and continues speaking, waving a hand as she does so. "Do you know what's the one thing that persuaded me to keep going?"

I shrug. If I'm at a loss, I can only imagine what TeeKay must have thought.

The waiter puts two beers on the table and takes the empty bottles away. Madz ashes her ciggie. The stack of ash collapses like an overwrought diva.

The tourist couple are across the street from us now, looking through the window of a tattoo parlour at a girl getting her navel pierced. She winces and they Ooh, and start debating again. The wife pulls out a notepad from her messenger bag and starts to write.

I turn back to Madz, who is examining her beer. She lowers her head to follow a drop of condensation sliding down the bottle. Then in a single motion she picks up the bottle and chugs down a third.

"What?" she says.

"You seem different, that's all."

"Different how?" she says.

"I don't know," I say. "Harder and more in danger."

"You mean dangerous?"

"I mean in danger, like you're just a fleeting thought."

"This is why I'm speaking to you, my friend. You get me," she says.

She snuffs out the cigarette and puts the one behind her ear in her mouth. She fishes out another from the box and replaces the one that was behind her ear.

"Madz," I say, "I'm telling you you've changed because I'm worried."

She lights the cigarette and lets it hang limply from her lips. She strums the table. I'm mothering her again.

"Okay," I say, "just tell me what made you keep on not showering."

"It's weird," Madz says, "but the longer I didn't shower, the clearer the memory of being clean became. Like, while my outside got grimy, my inside became clean. I was doing something important. I just knew it."

Her voice trails off. She fiddles with the lighter, spinning it around her fingers.

She says, "TeeKay didn't say one word. She'd come home every night and find me in the studio reeking. And nothing. Not a word. At night, she'd crawl into bed and pull me closer, no compunction."

"Were you testing her?" I say.

"I don't know what I was doing, but I knew it was important."

"So if she didn't mind any of it, why'd TeeKay dump you?"

Madz shakes her head. "It's not that simple," she says.

She takes a long drag of her ciggie and blows the smoke out the side of her mouth. She pulls herself out of a slouch, sits erect and leans in.

She says, "We were in Port Alfred last month, at someone's holiday home. You know what TeeKay's gallery friends are like, all pills and pretence."

"Don't I know it," I say. "That's also why I never liked her for you."

A tiny smirk appears at the corner of Madz's lips.

"Anyway," she says, "on the first night she got it into her head from nowhere that I had a thing for this rail-thin blonde. She got, like, crazy jealous. It put me off."

She rests her elbows on the table and leans in closer.

"On the third night," she says, "the mozzies kept me awake. It was so muggy that my skin felt like crude oil. I crept out of bed and walked down to the beach. It was completely dark. I only found the beach by following the sound of the waves. Dee, I can't explain it. The second I stepped onto the sand with my bare feet, I felt compelled to wade into the water. And I did, with all my clothes on. Then I swam out into the darkness as far as I could until it all felt like a dream. I think I blacked out."

I must have an astonished look on my face because Madz rubs my hand. It's consoling.

"I know, crazy," she says. "I woke up on the beach the next morning and TeeKay was in a state when I got back to the house. She said there was something different about me."

"Maybe because you'd finally had a bath," I venture.

She laughs a full laugh, the first since we've been here.

She says, "TeeKay refused to believe that I was at the beach alone and said she couldn't stand the change she saw in me. She said only one thing could change a person overnight and that was sex. I thought, after God knows how long of living with my stink, she's finally found her way out."

I nod. "Or maybe it's what you said," I say. "Maybe the outside is the inverse of the inside or something. Maybe after your swim, you looked filthy to her."

"Dee, my friend, this is why I am talking to you," Madz says. She reaches toward me, clasps her fingers around the back of my neck and pulls me to her. I feel her warm breath first, then her lips, soft against my forehead.

Everything disappears. A warm, woolly silence engulfs me and time seems to pause. Then slowly, it ebbs back. The door chime of the café, a scooter racing by on the street. In the distance, one of the *bergies* is awake. He shouts to a woman, "Hey madam, sorry pretty lady …" The tourist couple have taken a seat at the table next to us. When I notice them, they trade furtive glances. She quickly closes her notebook and slips it into her bag. He puts the lens cap back on his camera and pretends not to have been taking photos of us.

IMPEPHO

ROGER DIAMOND

I am at home. Summer in the Cape is warm and breezy. People are down on the beach or out on the mountain, hiking, climbing. I strike a match and set fire to a small bunch of twigs with grey leaves, then blow it out immediately and let the bunch smoulder. Siya did this here. Siya did lots of things here. We did lots of things together. And sometimes Siya did too much. Like too many drinks, too late, too fast. Who knows exactly what happened, but one night out drinking with friends he never made it home.

I look at the *impepho* smoke rising up to the ceiling, trying to get out to the sky, and I remember the first time Siya showed me what *impepho* was.

The bead of sweat dropped through the air, sparkling in the sharp morning sunlight, flung free from Siya's hair as he looked down at the city. I thought I could see the skyscrapers of Cape Town reflected upside-down in this micro-world, but it was probably just a mirage in my own dizzied brain from the heavy load and steep hike up. The drop's fall ended in silence, a miniscule wet spot on the grey quartzite on the path up Table Mountain. Years ago, path builders had laid these slabs here. I was shocked at how quickly something could pass from inside Siya's body, through the dark magma, escape, take flight, and end up on the rough rock, an insignificant speck of moisture on this ancient mountain.

Siya looked up at me and smiled, his body stooped and weary from the walk up the relentless path under the cableway. But his eyes were darting around at everything new. My heart pounded and my thighs burned as the tourists glided past above us in the cable car. Siya threw them a wounded glance as he panted for breath. We sat on a boulder to rest.

I usually get lost in the scenery when I climb, but this time my senses were occupied with Siya's breathing, his heat, and the smell of his sweat. I caught his eyes on my thigh and looked down at the blonde tendrils of my hair. I liked them, but they only get this way after lots of time in the sun, usually at the end of summer. They were waving in all directions from the rubbing of my shorts as we'd hiked. How different they were to the dense black curls on Siya's head, or to the smooth skin of his thighs, bulging from the exertion to get this far up the mountain. You could ponder our contrasting appearances indefinitely, throw science at them, or just bask in the glorious difference.

"Do we have to go on?" Siya asked. He was tired from a late night out. He knew we *had* a climb planned, I thought. But then, he had made the effort to get up in time.

"The tough bit is almost over and the fun will start soon," I promised.

And soon enough we got to the base of the cliff. We were both sweltering in the heat of the still morning and we stripped off our shirts. I fumbled with the ropes. My eyes couldn't let go of Siya's body, and I was tempted to ditch the climb and just be with him on the mountain.

"Ooh, what's this?" Siya grabbed a camelot, a climbing device that with much imagination has a penis shape. He shoved it in the direction of my butt, jabbing it into me. We laughed and hugged as

I dropped the pile of gear for a moment. I grabbed a set of nuts, metal chocks that have a distant likeness to testicles, and held them at his groin.

"Whoah, you've grown a few extras!" I said.

We were laughing, but then our eyes met and held. We stood still, nearly naked, close enough to touch, yet neither of us moved or spoke. I felt my soul being sucked into Siya's eyes. I could not feel my body and I had no thoughts – even the heat, the mountain and the day vanished in that moment.

But we were here to hike, right?

"Right, you're on belay," I said, and I clipped the ropes to my harness. "Climb when ready!" So Siya led up the first, easy pitch. In the ideal, calm weather I could talk him through any tricky parts and help him set up the belay at the top, where he would have to tie himself into the rock using pieces of gear that fit into the cracks.

"It's occupied," he called down when he reached the belay ledge. I was puzzled. I hadn't seen anyone up there. "By one of your friends!"

I laughed. Siya often referred to little critters like millipedes and geckos as "your friends" as I am such a lover of the non-human world. "What've you found?"

"One of those black lizards with the spikes. Not the queeny ones with colours."

"Once you've converted them too, tell me when you've set up the belay," I shouted up.

Within an hour we were on the lunch ledge. From here, you see eye to eye with the tourists crammed into the cable car, enjoying their spectacular but brief suspended existence on their way up or down the mountain. Siya was glowing. His envy of the lazy tourists was replaced with an obvious satisfaction that he was going up the mountain the real way.

Being so engaged with the very rock mass that forms this monolith at the tip of Africa is like plugging yourself into the earth's eternal energy and existence. I felt euphoric as we relaxed in the relative comfort of the wide, flat rock ledge, the euphoria of being utterly human, using both body and mind to overcome a natural challenge, this vertical dance of life we clinically call rock climbing. And when Siya and I allowed our bodies to join, becoming as close to one human as two people could, the euphoria became ecstasy.

I leant over and laid my head down on Siya's thigh, closed my eyes as he put his hand on me, and, hearing only his breathing, I drifted into quiet bliss.

A shriek interrupted my reverie.

"Impepho!" Siya shouted. I sat up and he scrambled across the ledge to where a small shrub was happily growing. *Impepho* is the Xhosa word for a grey helichrysum, a member of the daisy family with pungent leaves and a musky, herbal smell. He broke off a handful of twigs and squashed a few leaves under my nose. I breathed in deeply but pulled my head back as the rich smell filled me. The *impepho* exuded its fragrance so strongly on that hot day. Combined with the scent of Siya's sweat and skin, it engulfed me.

"We use it to cast away the evil spirits in a house by smouldering it in a bowl," Siya informed me, clutching the bunch with pride.

After a long drink of water and a short bite to eat, we tackled the final rock wall. I led up the pitch and left Siya on the lunch ledge to belay me. He sang in Xhosa and danced gently while I enjoyed the easy climbing. His singing added a warm, happy dimension to my already rich sensory experience.

The final moves land you on a rather unpleasant, bushy ledge from where you can walk off the cliff and back down the mountain. Spiky restios, reeds that look more like punk hairdos, and tough-leaved protea shrubs with occasional dead branches are among the greenery that cloaks the ledge. These all gave off a gentle smell of shrubbery, but nothing like the intense aroma of the *impepho*.

"Off belay," I shouted to Siya below.

"Belay off," he returned.

"Climb when ready," I yelled.

As Siya came into view around a rock bulge, I smiled at the tufts of grey *impepho* sticking out of the top of his pants. I had carried the backpack up, and there were no pockets in those jogging shorts of mine that he so loved to borrow, so he had tucked the *impepho* under the shorts' elastic. It must be really scratchy, I thought, and hoped it would not tumble out as he moved through the various awkward positions that the climbing demanded. But every now and then he spared a hand to reposition the bundle.

From the city far below us, the drone of traffic was perpetual, cut by the odd motorbike. The occasional whirr of the cable car on its thick metal cables reminded me of the tourist mecca we happen to have been born into. What a privilege. The diversity of landscapes and scenery in the Cape is matched only by the diversity of cultures and people who live here.

Siya intoxicated me. His approach and attitude to life were so different to mine. Once, I got home soaked and feeling like a drowned rat, caught in a downpour on my cycle back from work. I thought he'd see me as a cold, wet, miserable thing to be dispatched to the bathroom, but it was as if he didn't notice anything different. I was home, safe, and we were together. That was all that mattered to him.

"Hey, what do I do here?" he called up, nearing the last, tricky move. It is not straightforward and there is a jutting rock nearby that you could swing into if you fell. A graze and a bruise would be the very least damage, something broken if you fell badly. So I told him to get his feet up high and reach up with his right hand for my left hand, which I could spare. I braced myself and tightened up the belay. The rocks got harder and the bushes got spikier around us. Even the blue of the sky went hard. Siya's hand was trembling and the sweat was rolling off his chest.

"Better wipe your hand dry," I said.

He started up the overhanging block and reached up to the first grip. He sent me a quick glance as his eyes darted around looking for the next grips. Then he got his feet up and I could see his whole body, shaking now, his muscular mass reaching towards me. The *impepho* had nearly fallen out of his pants. It was hanging in front of his groin by a leaf or two. I had to do something to save it, but my feet were bracing my body, my one hand was on the rope and the other was holding the hand of my beloved. I dared not ask him anything or distract him from his delicate final moves.

Climbers are known for using their teeth. They are indispensible for holding gear or the rope while you're shifting your hands and getting your body into the right position, or selecting a piece of equipment. Teeth and jaws get a good workout on any decent climb. But the manoeuvre I was about to do was new to me. As Siya pulled on my hand and stepped up to my level, I leant crazily towards him and bit in the direction of the *impepho*. Ghampf!

"Whaa!?" Siya gasped.

I got the *impepho*. I got some loose shorts fabric. And I also got the soft flesh of Siya's penis. He lunged towards me and we collapsed into the bushes in a crazy bundle of rope, climbing gear, sweaty bodies and, somewhere in there, the *impepho*. Siya was quivering with relief, subsiding adrenalin and laughter, and I was grinning with happiness. I pulled my head away and dropped the *impepho*. Then, in a moment of delirious passion, I sunk my head back into his groin and he closed his thighs around me.

In there I felt dark, hot lava flowing all around me. Against my face his penis swelled with each pulse of his heart until I could feel that hard rod pressing from one end of my face to the other. I climbed out of his enclosure and we rearranged ourselves into an embrace. There we lay and kissed, bathing in the sun's rays. And the scent of two men, mixed with the fragrance of *impepho*, rose up to a serene blue sky.

ALL COVERED UP

DOLAR VASANI

It's January, one of the hottest months of the year. After a ten-hour flight from Geneva to Dar es Salaam, I'm about to embark on the final leg of my journey to the island of Zanzibar. Who would have thought I would return to Tanzania, the country of my birth, after almost thirty years? Definitely a perk of working for the United Nations.

In the small, shabby and rather stuffy airport lounge, I scan with some excitement the other passengers on my flight. A young woman with a black *abaya* and purple *hijab*, wearing Crocs, catches my attention. Cross-legged on the wooden bench, and chewing gum, she sways to the sounds blasting out of her iPod. But I am too tired to pay much heed. Everyone is immersed in their own thoughts. Most people are glued to their mobile phones, talking and texting. The tourists are engrossed in their guidebooks, contemplating the mysteries of the ancient spice island.

My final flight is only twenty minutes in a sixteen-seater Cessna. I grab a window seat and find the young woman in the black garb sitting next to me in the cramped and noisy cabin. We acknowledge and greet each other with our eyes. A film of perspiration covers my arms as I take another gulp of warm bottled water. Soon after takeoff, staring out at the expanse of the aquamarine Indian Ocean, I go in and out of consciousness. I want this hypnotic feeling to persist, but reality kicks in as the plane hits the tarmac of the bumpy runway.

When we disembark, the heat and humidity hit me like a bellowing fan. The swaying coconut trees in a sea of green vegetation, and the red earth, immediately infuse an air of exotic fantasy.

Walking out of the airport, I see the young woman from the plane; she smiles and strolls in the opposite direction. I allow myself to be distracted by her. But a stocky man with a goatee, chatting to the other taxi drivers, is holding a board with my name on it: DR CARMEN FERNANDEZ. He's elegantly dressed in a *kanzu* and a small white hat with elaborate embroidery. He extends his hand and says, "Karibu, Dr Carmen."

As we drive through the narrow lanes of Stone Town, he enquires about my flight and starts to reel off his frustrations about the endless power cuts. "We had the same problem last year. This is the third month without electricity. It's really terrible for the tourist industry." He continues his liberal venting until he drops me outside a white-painted, stone building covered with draping electricity cables, with open arched windows.

A dark stairway welcomes me to this government office in an historic old building. In a dank, hot room, my eyes take in the stacked box files and randomly strewn books. The chaos jolts my mind, making me question the seriousness of the work at hand. Several people are sitting around a long rectangular table, fanning themselves with papers. The ceiling fans remain motionless and the street noise penetrates the openings. All the women are dressed in black *abayas* and colourful *hijabs*. While we're exchanging polite pleasantries, the solid wooden door opens and in strolls a tall woman. She has a powerful aura, almost like a halo, and all heads turn towards her. She approaches me, extends her hand and confidently introduces herself. "Salama, I'm Yasmin Ahmed, Director of Planning." Her eyes are a hue of total black and there is a gap between her two front teeth, giving her a powerful yet playful disposition. Dripping in gold – rings, bangles, and earrings – she sits at the head of the table and declares the meeting officially open.

Shuffling papers, she scans my CV and looks over her reading glasses perched on her regal hooked nose. When she comments about the importance of returning to one's roots, I'm not sure what to say, wondering if it's an invitation to speak. She continues, "Karibu tena nyumbani. I see you were born here," and scans the room to check if everyone is present. Just then, in walks the last delegate.

Yasmin chuckles. "Dr Fernandez," she says, "this is Fatma, your escort. She'll take care of all your needs. You remember her from the emails?" I recall being amused by the symbols Fatma used to sign off her emails. The word escort stirs my imagination, and I wonder if this is what Zanzibari hospitality means.

"Asante sana. That's great and will be very helpful," I reply. Fatma smiles and winks at me, and our eyes lock in a disconcerting, fixed gaze. I find it alluring and start wondering how the week will pan out. It might be fun after all.

Yasmin keeps adjusting her floppy red scarf, showcasing her slender fingers, glittering with gold, smiling with her thick, bow-shaped eyebrows. Each time she smiles, her left cheek awakens with a gentlest of indentations. My mind starts to wonder how her hair looks without the *hijab*. I slowly veer into a space I never contemplated here, and I struggle to keep focused on the work at hand.

Before drawing the meeting to a close, Yasmin extends her business card and says, "Good luck with your assignment Dr Carmen. Call me if you need anything." I wonder if all business meetings in Zanzibar are filled with such mischief.

After the meeting, Fatma and I go out for a late lunch. In the bustling maze of Stone Town, hawkers ply their wares of scarves, nuts, CDs and carvings, spotting me, a foreigner, a mile away. We end up at the Archipelago, a rooftop restaurant overlooking the ocean.

Fronds of the coconut palms fan the air surrounding the verandah. Fishermen down below are chatting as they unload their daily catch from their dhows.

"How lovely to be away from the European winter and feel the warmth of the sun again," I say.

Fatma, in her cool manner, secures a corner table offering privacy and quietness. The staff draped in colonial-style, starched white aprons scurry around organising and serving our Swahili spicy crab curry. Fatma and I chat about the work assignment and appointments for the coming days.

She is slight and looks to be in her early thirties, although it's not easy to tell when so much of her is covered. She looks at me with her dark, almond-shaped eyes, which boast confidence and also exude gentleness. Her eyebrows are perfectly curved, giving her a strong appearance. She asks why I left Tanzania and if I ever think about returning. I jabber about everything and nothing, struggling to keep the conversation focused on work. Looking me in the eye, she responds, "I can see it's not easy after so many years," and waves her long and slender fingers, drawing the waiter's attention.

Feeling tired from the long journey, I welcome having an early night. Fatma walks me to the Tembo Hotel, located on the seafront and offering much needed respite from the soaring summer temperatures. She departs, leaving the softest peck infused with the subtle scent of lemongrass on my cheek. From my verandah, I watch the sun dipping under the shimmering waves of the Indian Ocean, and bask in the warmth of this corner of East Africa.

The following days, Fatma and I interview different government officials in their dilapidated hovels as part of my programme formulation mission. On Thursday afternoon, during one such meeting in another hot and airless room, she passes me a note: THIS IS BORING,

LET'S GO. Once out, she hails a taxi, and once in it, we collapse in a fit of giggles.

She says, "I'm tired of listening to the same blah, blah."

I welcome the unexpected distraction and wonder what she has planned.

We head northwards towards some place that is meaningless to me. She haggles with the driver about the price, which is common practice here. I gaze mindlessly out of the window at the coconut and spice farms. Fatma's scent is pervasive, awakening my fantasies. My tenderness towards her is growing and, while I want to freeze this moment, this feeling of excitement, I also start to wonder what she may think of me.

At one point, I catch her staring at me and she says, "Carmen, you have the most distinguished way of tying your hair. Do you ever wear it loose?"

I fumble and mutter something inane about it being easier in this climate. My mouth is increasingly dry, and a lump in my throat silences me from any further contributions. All I want to do is to grab her and kiss her. Does she know that I am at least ten years older than her and is that even important?

Distracted and locked in my own space, I don't realise the car has stopped and Fatma is asking me to step out. We walk silently on the powdery white sand towards the coconut sellers. The sea air is refreshing and a welcome relief from the sparks that are beginning to ignite between us.

In the taxi on the way back from the beach, Fatma's hand glides across the back seat and she starts playing with my fingers. I cannot look at her, and I just enjoy the tactile contact. Her forwardness is titillating and a shock to my system, forcing me to challenge all my preconceived notions and stereotypes. I continue staring out of the window feeling goose bumps all over my body and electric pulsations between my legs. I wonder what she may be thinking and if her skin is also prickling under the *abaya*. I am relieved to be dropped off at the hotel, needing time to think over the events of the day and make some sense of it all.

Tembo Hotel is steeped in history, furnished with oriental and traditional Zanzibari ornaments and antiques. At the centre of the courtyard is an azure blue swimming pool offering a perfect cool-off from the heat of the day. I climb the narrow wooden stairs to my room, and relish spending time on my balcony witnessing the commotion below – boys playing football on the beach, hawkers harassing tourists, and the daily mayhem of loading up the ferry.

Feeling the glow from the hues of orange and soft yellows of another perfect sunset, I retire to my giant, hand-carved, four-poster Zanzibari bed for a power nap. Just then, I receive a text message: HOPE YOUR BED IS COMFORTABLE. LALA SALAMA. YASMIN. Not knowing how to interpret this, I reply with a couple of smileys.

I've dozed off when the phone rings, making me jump. It's Fatma wondering what I'm doing stuck in my room. "Come and join me at Forodhani, it's only five minutes from your hotel." We agree to meet at the fountain around nine-ish. I spend more time than ever getting ready, selecting and discarding the entire contents of my suitcase. Staring in the mirror, I splash water to cool my frayed nerves and talk to myself. I walk out, butterflies in my stomach, but excited as a lovesick teenager.

Forodhani Park is bustling with activity. Local people and tourists are in abundance, exploring the food stalls and enjoying the sea breeze and evening light. Children scurry in all directions and a handsome crowd gathers to watch young men dive off the jetty. For the first time, Fatma is wearing a tight-fitting, short-sleeved top, exposing her smooth arms and the defined curves of her body. Her head remains covered. She's oozing sex appeal and I cannot stop ogling.

"Mambo vipi," she says, holding my hand with her baby-soft fingers and smiling impishly.

"Good evening, it's nice to get out. What an amazing setting," I remark.

Fatma is popular and chats to many people. Greetings are important here and people have a lot of time for each other. With Zanzibar pizza and sugar cane juice in hand, we park ourselves on a circular concrete bench and watch the world pass by.

A group of young women approach us and start chatting and giggling with Fatma. I wonder if they can sense my hankering for their friend. I say little and enjoy being the casual observer. Before long, a Vespa scooter stops across the road and a tall, bearded man in his thirties joins us. He extends his hand and quietly introduces himself as Abu. He talks to Fatma in Swahili and she goes across the road with him. Without further ado, Fatma puts on a helmet and plants herself side-saddle, departing on the back of Abu's *pikipiki.* It all happens too fast for me to work out the social dynamics. All I know is that I have a leaking crotch and my body temperature is rising.

As I walk back to the hotel, I replay the scenes, trying to unravel the puzzle. Who exactly is Abu? A boyfriend, brother, uncle, husband? Have I misinterpreted everything? Perhaps I've been reading too much into things. My nervous flutter calms down, and for my sanity I decide to let it be. It's time to refocus and concentrate on finishing my assignment.

The heat and clamminess are relentless. I put the ceiling fan on maximum, grab an ice-cold Coke, switch on the TV, and cool off under a shower.

While I'm drying my hair, I hear about Uganda's proposed anti-homosexuality bill on the BBC and I cannot believe my ears. My phone beeps. THINKING OF YOU. SWEET DREAMS. KISS. FXXX, the text message from Fatma reads. Her tone and suggestive intentions send tingles all over my hot body. Without making any assumptions, I reply with a whole line of smileys. I sleep absorbed by thoughts of her pouty, seductive lips, and I let my fingers stimulate my engorged pussy, releasing my pent-up sexual desires.

It's my last day and time for our final wrap-up session with Yasmin and a handful of other delegates from various ministries. We meet in the same dreary meeting room as on the first day. Yasmin is wearing an orange *hijab* and smiling from ear to ear, being very chatty, and asking many questions throughout the meeting. Her stares at me are relentless. While I find it amusing, it's also unsettling. I wonder what the others might be thinking. Fatma asks the odd question here and there. Everyone else is sitting quietly observing Yasmin's antics. I keep thinking about fast-tracking all inputs and wrapping things up quickly.

Mid-morning, we gather outside to say our goodbyes. Yasmin holds onto my arm and gives me an extended peck on the cheek. "Thank you for coming. I hope your next mission will be before Ramadan." Her perfume is overpowering yet seductive. While I enjoy the endless flirting and innuendos, I force myself to remain calm and keep everything very professional.

"Thank you for your wonderful hospitality, Yasmin. I will send you the final report by email," I assure her.

Fatma extends her hand. "I enjoyed spending time with you, Doctor. Hope you have a good trip back." It's done calmly, almost coldly. I don't dwell on it.

I leave alone with the driver and head back to the hotel in the government four-by-four to finish packing, wondering how the next few hours will unfold. In my room, I throw off my shoes and jacket. I try to stay calm, but I cannot sit still. I pace up and down, checking myself in the mirror. My mind is racing and my nerves are ricocheting randomly in nervous excitement. The time passes at a snail's pace.

There is a knock on the door. My heart starts racing and my hands are moist with anticipation. My mouth is parched, and I take a few deep breaths before opening the door. Fatma is standing there with one hand on her hip and holding a cell phone in the other.

"I think this belongs to you. You left it in the meeting room," she says with her laughing eyes.

I stand there motionless and in disbelief. I repeatedly comb my hair with my trembling fingers and unconvincingly say, "Oh, did I? I didn't know it was missing." She stands there patiently, waiting to be invited, and after a few more awkward, silent moments, fumbling, I invite her in.

With minimal eye contact, she walks into the room and like a magnetic surge heads straight to the open balcony. "Mmmm, nice view," she says, exposing her arms as she grips the latticed wooden railings.

There seems to be a giant marble in my mouth as I say, "Yes. Pity I can't stay longer to explore it."

I try hiding my nervous excitement and seek solace in the bathroom. I close the door to gather my thoughts. My knees are shaking and my breasts have tightened. I stare in the mirror and randomly blabber to myself, Fuck! What do I do? I can't ever remember feeling so lustful over someone I hardly know. I wipe the sweat off my face, tie back my damp hair, take in a few more deep breaths, and head back into the bedroom contemplating the next move.

Fatma is still on the balcony shaking her head and scratching her hair. "What a relief! It's too hot!" she exclaims.

Feeling alive with a pulsating heart, I instinctively blurt out, "Wow, what beautiful hair. So many curls," unsure how that came out or whether it's appropriate or not. I try to regain my composure and ask if she'd like a drink.

She pulls me towards her and whispers, nibbling my ear. "I don't want a drink Carmen, I want you."

The next few hours are a haze.

Fatma kisses my moist neck. Her lemongrass scent drives me wild. My breasts and wet pussy tighten with excitement. We giggle, and before long the tips of our tongues meet. I yearn to probe her mouth and full lips.

Holding her close, I say, "I've been wanting to kiss you since the first day." I clasp her face in my hand. I stroke her hair and plant my hungry tongue inside her mouth. She unties my hair band and starts playing with my damp mop. My curiosity to explore her body is overwhelming and my hands start discovering this uncharted and hidden territory. "I've never navigated a *buibui* before," I say, as I impatiently and hurriedly undress her. "Gosh Fatma, you are mysterious."

Her beautiful silky body is clad in sexy lacy lingerie and she has a henna tattoo across her abdomen. Having enjoyed being hunted, I elect to dominate my prey by holding her wrists firmly above her head on the Zanzi-bed and devouring her from head to toe. I lick the contours of her cinnamon-toned and taut body. I caress her mango-like breasts, slowly tickling her hardened nipples. She throws her head back and starts squealing. Mounting her, my hands enter her silky panties, finding a swollen pussy that is gushing and pulsating. My fingers start caressing her labia and stroking her soft clit. She moans as I rub her, increasing in force and speed. She wiggles her hips as I go down and taste her beyond her rough tuft of pubic hair. When I'm sucking her with my tongue, she grabs my head and holds it in place. I feel her whole body shudder as she screams and ejaculates, releasing all into my mouth. I cradle her in my arms, wishing this feeling of togetherness to be eternal.

Fatma strokes my drenched body with her long slender fingers, kissing me hard and long. Her assertive tongue explores every corner of my mouth. She slowly makes her way to my ears and sucks my lobes and whispers, "Carmen, how shall I fuck you?" I let her squat on my belly and ride me with strong thrusts. Her other hand tickles one erect nipple and she continues thrusting her tongue down my throat until I purr. Her long fingers enter my wet and waiting pussy. My clit is sensitive and wavy contractions permeate my whole body. I have an overwhelming desire to be taken and I let her continue her mischievous dominance. Playfully, she turns me onto my belly and starts massaging my back. Her strong yet soft hands knead into every inch of my body and she enters me again.

"You taste exactly like I thought," she says, and continues with her slender fingers, stroking me till I let out a bark of pleasure.

We lie in each others arms, exhausted, content and bewildered. I make a comment about highlighting this activity in my trip report. We giggle and start another round of mutual exploration.

I casually ask about Yasmin, and about Abu. Fatma laughs and says, "You ask too many questions and read too much into things."

Unsatisfied with her answer, I say, "Okay, one last question. What would you have done if I hadn't left my phone behind?"

Fatma smiles and chuckles. "Hmm, I had my own plan, Dr Fernandez. I will just have to try it another time."

Later, on the plane, I sit exhausted and in amazement at the serendipitous experience. Fatma's scent is in my hair and all over my body. I wonder if anyone else can smell the sex on me. I want to sustain this feeling in my throbbing pussy all the way back to freezing Switzerland.

THE FILTH OF FREEDOM

RAHIEM WHISGARY

James Drummond doesn't dream of a dutiful and loving wife by his side, a warm home, with laughing children and a furry brown dog leisurely curled up at the foot of the couch. Nor does he dream, as is more common with those of his young age, of jetting around the world, of experiencing the rapidity of New York, the pubs in London; of being awed by the technology of Hong Kong, or perhaps the pyramids at Giza, or the stony, idyllic beauty of Greece. No. Engulfed in the warmth of his down-feather duvet, smothered by the comforting quiet of the night, James dreams of his death.

The despotic, unchallenged laws of the universe will ensure that, once again, in a mere few hours the sun will rise, bringing with it all the problems of his world, from which James wishes to hide. His stomach turns to rock, and he curls up into a bony question mark, hardly able to withstand the pain yet not wishing it away. He basks in it, feeds it with thoughts of the futility of struggling through life, the inability ever to find true happiness, the dreary nightmare of being content with one's lot, and the terror of being alone forever, never being found attractive, desirable, wanted. Yet it is only within this warmth and comfort, in the privacy and security of his dark room, that James relishes his negativity. In the light of day, it is plain to him, as it is to those around him, that his fears are not unfounded, and that he needs to make a plan.

Making a plan is simple. Alone in the night, it is easy to string up a concurrent series of small events that will gain James access to the necessary material to achieve his goal, particularly as it concerns only himself. It is the execution of the plan that will be the challenge. But he is not a coward. He may be slight in build, tentative and shy, and he certainly prefers his own company, but given the right motivation, James could accomplish his goal. He is as sure of that as he is sure that he wants to die on his own terms.

James rises from his bed like a cautious snail emerging from its shell. Rummaging in a drawer at his bedside, he finds, among the scraps of paper, the empty bottles of moisturiser and cans of deodorant, the long-expired condoms neatly tucked in their wrappers, a cigarette box still containing half its original contents. Removing one cigarette and a bright red lighter, he reburies the box in the debris. Social ills have always been hushed in the Drummond family and, as much as possible, concealed from outsiders. One never spoke about Uncle Gary's excessive drinking, or Althea's abortion; and not even a mention of Mr Drummond's affection for his black protégé. Smoking definitely falls in this category and James dare not draw attention to his habit, even though he is quite sure his parents are silently aware of it.

Sitting at the foot of his bed, in black boxer shorts, he opens the window, letting in a chilly breeze. With one foot on the bed and the other on the furry warmth of the cream carpet, James lights his cigarette and takes a long puff. Then he rests his wrist on the windowpane, the cigarette between his fingers lingering outside the window. The breeze tousles his detested dark hair and spitefully redirects the smoke into the room.

It is not often that he wakes in the early hours of the morning, and it is even rarer that he has actually gotten out of bed. But there is something simmering in him. At his core, underneath his negativity, underneath his self-pity, is something strange: a spark, threatening the beginning of something bigger. He cannot ignore the feeling, but he doesn't know what to do with it. It has lifted him from complacency and given him a small sense of vigour, of vitality – but to what purpose?

Taking another long draw, James drops his eyes to gaze from his second storey window beyond the boundary wall to the street below. As is usual with suburbs in Johannesburg, the street lamps are out and the street devoid of life. The tall, old trees add to the deserted, ghostly feel, and it seems to James that he's looking in on the set of a horror movie. He flicks his cigarette stub out of the window and watches as it falls to the dark lawn.

The stub dissolves into the night, but the thought of it lying there in the light of day, its muted yellow colour visible among the manicured blades of grass, gives James a thrill, a sense of malicious excitement. He knows that, just as the sun begins to rise, Margaret, his family's domestic worker, will hobble from her quarters at the back of the property across the lawn to ensure that breakfast is ready when the family wakes. She will surely notice the cigarette stub, and, to avoid the perpetuation of the antagonism between Thabo, her son, and James, she will dispose of it, ensuring that Mr and Mrs Drummond never have to set their eyes on such evidence.

Thabo, despite growing up in the Drummond household and being just a year younger than James's eighteen, has none of James's refined tastes or mannerisms. Thabo was the boy who would gladly kick a ball in the garden with Mr Drummond, while James preferred to recline in the shade of a tree, engrossed in the fictional and fantastic lives of characters in a novel. Thabo has grown up to be the son with whom Mr Drummond can share his views on the state of South African rugby, the son Mr Drummond can consult about difficult business decisions. Margaret has been the dutiful employee of the Drummond family since five years before Thabo's birth. The Drummond couple, delighted that their own son, James, now had a "brother", always saw to Thabo's education, his clothes and stationery. Thabo lived with his mother in the back, in the two-roomed residence with adjoining bathroom, but he grew up a part of the Drummond family, attending the same school as James, often having supper with the family and being present at family outings and holidays. Of course, Margaret was always invited; and she always declined. But it filled her with joy that her son would never have to live in the poverty she knew.

Knowing that he'll be unable to go back to sleep, James finds another cigarette and takes his place at the window again. The cool breeze livens his skin with a thin layer of goose pimples. His mind moves from one possibility to the next, complicating what initially seemed an easy solution. He gives up, flicks his second cigarette stub down to the grass, closes the window, and snuggles under the covers.

His mind, still too alive for sleep, floats from one nude image to another: beautifully sculpted males, in black and white, posing suggestively yet modestly, each positioned on a strong rectangular stone, all secretly tempting him with the arch of a foot, the subtle flex of a thigh, the slight exposure of a neck. Colour seeps into the scene, and James stands in a magnificent room made of large stone bricks. He taunts the nudes with his coy resistance, his seeming indifference. He is not a puppy they can lure with a whistle, a simple call, a show of meat. One by one, his nudes, all blonde, all so perfectly sculpted from sun-kissed rock, turn to face him. They are the epitome of Aryan male beauty – as is James, whose normally large nose is transformed into a narrow, dainty feature, his dark hair dramatically lightened to gold, his mother's strong Jewish heritage entirely erased from his being. He smiles, lifting both his arms in a show of grandeur and excitement at the presence of such beauty. He doesn't wear a crown – that would be too tacky – but the rich, blood red fabrics swathing his body are testimony to his royalty. He is king, a young beautiful Aryan king, answerable to no one but God.

His bouncing hand is creating a bulging hill in the duvet, and in his mind he slowly beckons his nudes towards him. They oblige but are in no hurry, almost swaggering, with a hint of defiance in their eyes. His hand stops moving: each perfect nude carries a live chicken at his side; each has a powerful hand clasped around a struggling bird's neck. James's eyes shoot open, alive and disgusted, revealing their true dark brilliance. Physically willing the images away, he violently turns on his side, hating mankind, hating himself, feeling dirty – not physically, not even mentally, but dirty on the inside, under his skin. He longs to plunge a knife into his scrawny chest and drag it downwards, allowing his polluted insides to fall out. He drifts off into a restless sleep, curled into his question mark.

When the detested beams of yellow light wake James up, highlighting the suspended dust particles in their hovering dance, he turns his back: if he can't see it, then it doesn't exist. Oblivious to the faint smell of burnt tobacco that has tainted the caged air in his room, he lulls himself back into slumber.

Two rude raps on the wooden door, then it flies open and Thabo strides in. He is wearing loose-fitting, washed-out blue jeans, sneakers and a light blue T-shirt, which contrasts horribly with his dark complexion.

"James. Your mother says you to have help me clean the pool."

James turns away from Thabo but, confronted by the sunrays, he irritably turns back.

"I wouldn't make her wait too long if I were you. She's not in a very good mood."

With the sudden alertness of a snoozing kitten spotting a lone rolling ball, James sees, in the doorway, on the floor, two small yellow rolls of paper: his cigarette stubs of last night. They seem spent and alone in their uselessness, pieces of trash on off-white porcelain tiles, but to James they mean acknowledgement: acknowledgement of his faults, of his disobedience, of his dishonour, not only to himself but to his family, to his parents. To flout his sordid habit, to not even have the decency to hide it, do it undercover or at least lie … there is bound to be retribution.

Motionless in his bed, feeling a stirring in his stomach, staring at the stubs, James instantly craves a cigarette. Instead he turns to Thabo, who is looking smugly at him from his position against the wall.

"Is she angry?" says James.

"She hasn't said anything."

Icy and still, his feet too heavy to move and his heart booming against his ribcage, James feels he's on the brink of fainting. The underlying steel of his mother's placid demeanour makes him tremble. Her narrowed eyes, her pouted lips and clipped tone, easily reveal her mood, and with no need to mention the transgression, she piles on the punishment in heaps of chores and petulant disregard. But it's not her coldness that terrifies James. It is the knowledge that very soon the taut string that is Mrs Drummond's anger will snap. Nobody knows when it will happen, and James is perpetually treading on eggshells.

Unable to ignore James's obvious dread, Thabo, fighting the smile on his face, picks up the stubs and places them on the cabinet next to the bed. "I think you should throw these away."

Allowing the facts to sink in, James marinades under the covers for a few moments longer. Then, with a sharp inhale, he sits up, feet planted in the softness of the carpet, facing Thabo.

"Who put them there?" he asks, indicating the doorway. His voice is not strained, but it is clear that battle lines have been drawn.

"I did," Thabo says.

James's hands clench. Consumed with a malicious rage, his abdomen caves in and his back rounds like the shell of a beetle. With a slow exhale, his eyes open to meet Thabo's. "Why?"

Thabo paces back and forth against the length of the wall like an invigilating teacher, his substantial weight leaving behind him defined prints in the soft carpet. "So they don't think it's me that smokes."

James springs up with an electrifying jolt. "But you couldn't just have thrown them away?"

"No."

All the years of competition, of failing, of falling, come flooding into James: Thabo, secure in his erudite masculinity, achieving on the sports field as well as academically. Thabo, able, like Mr and Mrs Drummond, to wash over the passionate shades of red, purple and black in their lives with a more neutral beige. Thabo, who doesn't have anything to hide, no secret fantasies. Thabo, who is complacent in the mediocrity of life, of obeying, of achieving to the established benchmarks rather than setting his own. Thabo, who constantly feels the need to be better than James.

James's dark eyes pierce Thabo's. "Why? I want to know why."

Thabo gestures with his arms as he speaks. It is an effort to remain nonchalant, but his underlying disgust shines through and his movements only serve to dramatise what he says. "Because you're a faggot."

Whether Thabo means it as a slur on James's sexual preference or as an insult alluding to James's ineptness, James does not know. But Thabo has hit a nerve. James's blood courses through his body, blinding his sight. The sinews in his neck push out against his pale skin, causing the muscles along his shoulders, down his upper back and arms to clench. He crouches briefly and then charges at Thabo, as surprising as a bolt of lightning. Thabo finds himself pinned between the wall and James's near-naked body. James's right hand is on Thabo's throat, and James, centimetres from Thabo's face, consumed by a bloodied anger, swings his left, weaker fist and makes contact with Thabo's jaw. Thabo retaliates instinctively, pushes James hard, causing him to stumble backwards and fall. Thabo steps between James's spread legs and pins him to the floor, his hand on James's neck. James's eyes bulge, initially out of surprise at being dominated so violently, and then because he is unable to inhale. Rasping sounds escape from his throat as Thabo, positioned over his body, moves closer to his face, so close that their lips seem to brush. Then Thabo lowers his crotch to make contact with James's. Stuttering through breathless speech, his arms desperately flailing at his side, James is unable to fight off the bigger boy. With all restraint now dissolved, Thabo punches James with his free hand. He leans in to speak.

"You are a faggot, aren't you?" This time, his use of the word is clear.

"Let go of my son!" a shrill voice screams behind them.

Immediately, Thabo releases his grip. James gasps for breath. With those two words – my son – Mrs Drummond has severed a tie that has taken seventeen years to bind. Treated equally, as her own son, Thabo has been more a part of the family than the reclusive James. And even though Thabo referred to her as Mrs Drummond, she is just as much a mother to him as Margaret is. But now, the distinction between himself, the maid's son, and Mrs Drummond's biological son, has been made. Thabo moves to leave the room.

Mrs Drummond stops him in the doorway. "James, get dressed. And both of you: to the pool. Now."

A feeling ignites in James: he is blood, and despite how much better Thabo is than James, blood is blood. His eyes drift towards the pathetic black boy standing pained and uncomfortable in his shabby working clothes, wanting to leave. The boy who has tried so hard to fit into a family that isn't his. So hard that he has almost dislodged the family's biological son. Superiority floats James, and he strides over to the cigarette stubs on the bedside cabinet and picks them up.

"He put these outside my door this morning, Mom."

Mrs Drummond's head begins to spin. She sees the boy who overachieved, who became closer to her husband than his own son.

She sees through his pure outer casing to his spiteful inside self. What she and her husband have done for Thabo is not good enough: he will only be satisfied once he's completely pushed James out. She turns her gaze from the stubs to Thabo. "Is this true?"

Everything inside Thabo sinks to the floor, and he answers with a dejected, "Yes. Yes, but–"

And Mrs Drummond's taut string snaps. "If it wasn't for pity of your mother, I'd kick you out of here right now! All morning I've been agonising over my son, my own child … I thought Margaret saw him smoking and it was Margaret who put them there to warn him, or warn me, or … but it was you, you trying to frame my boy and push him out even further. I am torn between slapping you myself, right here, and watching your mother give you the beating you deserve!"

However hard he longs, Thabo knows that he cannot wish Mr Drummond here. Mr Drummond disappears every second weekend to oversee a business he has on the east coast. Where Mr Drummond spends his nights while on those trips is anyone's guess. And no one dare ask, least of all Mrs Drummond.

Mrs Drummond meanders to her room, the dirty pool forgotten. She feels drunk on her sudden explosion of emotion, and shocked at her outburst. Without glancing at James, Thabo retreats from the room.

Thabo sits at his yellow pine desk. Mrs Drummond's words swirl around in his head. No matter how hard he works, how much of himself he stifles, he will never truly be part of the family, he will never truly be accepted by them. The stink of decaying dog shit wafts in from outside, reminding him of his place. He will never be their son.

He tears a sheet of paper from his notepad and begins to write.

A sneaky, ugly feeling creeps up on James. He assumed that defeating Thabo would feel powerful, that even though he lied to his mother, he would still feel dominant. Stripped of the grandeur of his kingly fantasies, James realises that everything is ugly at its core. He longs to go back to the moment when he told his lie, but would he have done anything differently? Faint from the guilt, he sits down on his bed. The room spins around him as he remembers what Thabo said just before his mother interrupted them. The words are ringing in his head now: You are a faggot, aren't you. It wasn't a question. More of a realisation, cruelly stating a fact.

Curling in on himself, James fiercely hugs his abdomen, his fingers pressing into the flesh at his sides. His jaw clenched to will back the tears, he lifts his head to look beyond the bland whiteness of the ceiling to the heavens. The tears spill. Even in his aloneness he feels a tinge of embarrassment and immediately wipes them away. Spitefully, the sunrays catch his naked back, and in a burst of emotion, James throws the cigarette stubs at the window. Bouncing off the glass, defeated, he watches them fall pathetically to the floor.

After a moment's hesitation, a moment of staring at the spent stubs, James pulls on jeans and a T-shirt. Tentatively, he opens the drawer and, staring him right in the face, in all its royal blue glory in the mess, is the cigarette box. James takes the box in his hand, slams the drawer shut, and strides out of the room. With a pacing confidence reminiscent of the medieval monarchs he so admires, James heads towards his mother's room, high on confidence, the impending freedom of being purged, of being honest. His mood, like his head, regardless of the looming consequences, rises higher and higher.

When he turns the corner to his parents' room, James sees his mother, frozen on the edge of her bed, a letter in her hand. Her dark hair falls around her, encasing her shoulders. She looks up at him, tears streaming down her face. She looks from his eyes to the cigarette box in his hand. The world stops in a moment of frozen tension. Everything in James floats to the surface, dead, like driftwood floundering on the ocean surf. Unable to make to a sound, he meets his mother's eyes. Both of them are defeated. In a weak gesture, she lifts the letter. "It's from Thabo," is all she can say.

And it's all James needs to hear. He knows the contents, the entire contents of the letter. In his cruel spitefulness, Thabo has gone beyond the truth of the cigarette incident.

A sinking feeling overtakes James and he turns and runs. His chest caves in as he stumbles along the corridor, down the stairs, and drunkenly staggers his way outside. Unaware of where he is going, of what to do, he simply needs to get out of the stifling bounds of the house. A gulp of fresh air fills his lungs as he steadies himself against the wall outside. His head spins, and he collapses onto his haunches, the thick grass cushioning him. Unsteadily, he takes a cigarette and the bright red lighter from the box. And before long, James inhales the smoky filth of freedom.

JAMBULA TREE

MONICA ARAC DE NYEKO

I heard of your return home from Mama Atim our next door neighbour. You remember her, don't you? We used to talk about her on our way to school, hand in hand, jumping, skipping, or playing run-and-catch-me. That woman's mouth worked at words like ants on a cob of maize. Ai! Everyone knows her quack-quack-quack mouth. But people are still left wordless by just how much she can shoot at and wreck things with her machinegun mouth. We nicknamed her "lecturer". The woman speaks with the certainty of a lecturer at her podium claiming an uncontested mastery of her subject.

I bet you are wondering how she got to know of your return. I could attempt a few guesses. Either way, it would not matter. I would be breaking a promise. I hate that. We made that promise never to mind her or be moved by her. We said that after that night. The one night no one could make us forget. You left without saying goodbye after that. You had to, I reasoned. Perhaps it was good for both of us. Maybe things could die down that way. Things never did die down. Our names became forever associated with the forbidden. Shame.

Anyango – Sanyu.

My mother has gotten over that night. It took a while, but she did. Maybe it is time for your mother to do the same. She should start to hold her head high and scatter dust at the women who laugh after her when she passes by their houses.

Nakawa Housing Estates has never changed. Mr Wangolo our SST teacher once said those houses were just planned slums with people with broken dreams and unplanned families for neighbours. Nakawa is still over one thousand families on an acre of land they call an estate. Most of the women don't work. Like Mama Atim they sit and talk, talk, talk and wait for their husbands to bring home a kilo of offal. Those are the kind of women we did not want to become. They bleached their skins with Mekako skin lightening soap till they became tender and pale like a sun-scorched baby. They took over their children's *dool* and *kwepena* catfights till the local councillor had to be called for arbitration. Then they did not talk to each other for a year. Nakawa's women laugh at each other for wearing the cheapest sandals on sale by the hawkers. Sanyu, those women know every love charm by heart and every ju-ju man's shrine because they need them to conjure up their husbands' love and penises from drinking places with smoking pipes filled with dried hen's throat artery. These women know that an even number is a bad sign as they watch the cowry shells and coffee beans fall onto cowhide when consulting the spirits about their husbands' fidelity.

That's what we fought against when we walked to school each day. Me and you hand in hand, towards school, running away from Nakawa Housing Estates' drifting tide which threatened to engulf us and turn us into noisy, gossiping and frightening housewives. You said it yourself, we could be anything. Anything coming from your mouth was seasoned and alive. You said it to me, as we sat on a mango tree branch. We were not allowed to climb trees, but we did, and there, inside the green branches, you said – we can be anything. You asked us to pause for a moment to make a wish. I was a nurse in a white dress. I did not frighten children with big injections. You wished for nothing. You just made a wish that you would not become what your father wanted you to be – an engineer, making building plans, for his mansion, for his office, for his railway village. The one he dreamt about when he went to bed at night.

Sanyu, after all these years, I still imagine shame trailing after me tagged onto the hem of my skirt. Other times, I see it, floating into your dreams across the desert and water, to remind you of what lines we crossed. The things we should not have done when the brightness of Mama Atim's torch shone upon us – naked. How did she know exactly when to flash the light? Perhaps asking that question is a futile quest for answers. I won't get any! Perhaps it is as simple as accepting that the woman knows everything. I swear if you slept with a crocodile under the ocean, she would know. She is the only one who knows first hand whose husband is sleeping with whose daughter at the estate, inside those one-bedroomed houses. She knows whose son was caught inside the fences at Lugogo Show Grounds, the fancy trade fair centre just across Jinja Road, the main road which meanders its way underneath the estate. Mama Atim knows who is soon dying from gonorrhoea, who got it from someone, who got it from so-and-so who in turn got it from the soldiers who used to guard Lugogo Show Grounds, two years ago.

You remember those soldiers, don't you? The way they sat in the sun with their green uniforms and guns hanging carelessly at their shoulders. With them the AK47 looked almost harmless – an object that was meant to be held close to the body – black ornament. They whistled after young girls in tight miniskirts that held onto their bums. At night, they drank Nile Lager, tonto, Mobuku and sang harambe, Soukous or Chaka Chaka songs.

Eh moto nawaka mama, Eh moto nawaka,
I newaka tororo, Nawaka moto
Nawaka moto, Nawaka moto

Eh fire, burns mama, Eh fire, burns
It is burning in Tororo, It is burning
It is burning, It is burning

Mama Atim never did pass anywhere near where they had camped in their green tents. She twisted her mouth when she talked about them. What were soldiers doing guarding Lugogo? she asked. Was it a frontline? Mama Atim was terrified of soldiers. We never did find out why they instilled such fear in her. Either way it did not matter. Her fear became a secret weapon we used as we imagined ourselves being like goddesses dictating her fate. In our goddess hands, we turned her into an effigy and had soldiers pelt her with stones. We imagined that pelting stones from a soldier was just enough to scare her into *susuing* in her XXL mother's union panties. The ones she got a tailor to hem for her, from leftover materials from her children's nappies. How we wished those materials were green, so that she would see soldiers and stones in between her thighs every time she wore her green soldier colour, stone pelting colour and AK47 colour.

We got used to the sight of green soldiers perched in our football fields. This was the new order. Soldiers doing policemen's work! No questions, Uganda *yetu*, *hakuna matata*. How strange it was, freedom in forbidden colours. Deep green – the colour of the morning when the dew dries on leaves to announce the arrival of shame and dirt. And everything suddenly seems so uncovered, so exposed, so naked.

Anyango – Sanyu.

Mama Atim tells me you have chosen to come back home, to Nakawa Housing Estates. She says you refuse to live in those areas on the bigger hills and terraced roads in Kololo. You are coming to us and to Nakawa Housing Estates, and to our many houses lined one after another on a small hill overlooking the market and Jinja Road, the football field and Lugogo Show Grounds. Sanyu, you have chosen to come here to children running on the red earth, in the morning shouting and yelling as they play *kwepena* and *dool* – familiar and stocked with memory and history. You return to dirt roads filled with thick brown mud on a rainy day, pools of water in every pothole and the sweet fresh smell of rain on hard soil. Sanyu, you have come back to find Mama Atim.

Mama Atim still waits for her husband to bring the food she is to cook each night. We used to say, After having nine sons and one daughter, she should try to take care of them. Why doesn't she try to find a job in the industrial area like many other women around the estate? Throw her hips and two large buttocks around and play at entrepreneurship. Why doesn't she borrow a little *entandikwa* from the micro finance unions so she can buy at least a bale of second-hand clothes at Owino market where she can retail them at Nakawa market? Second-hand clothes are in vogue, for sure. The Tommy Hilfiger and Versace labels are the "in-thing" for the young boys and girls who like to hang around the estate at night. Second-hand clothes never stay on the clothes hangers too long, like water during a drought, they sell quickly.

Mummy used to say those second-hand clothes were stripped off corpses in London. That is why they had slogans written on them such as – YOU WENT TO LONDON AND ALL YOU BROUGHT ME WAS THIS LOUSY T-SHIRT! When Mummy talked of London, we listened with our mouths open. She had travelled there not once, not twice, but three times to visit her sister. Each time she came back with her suitcase filled up with stories. When her sister died, Mummy's trips stopped like that bright sparkle in her eye and the Queen Elizabeth stories, which she lost the urge to retell again and again. By that time we were grown. You were long gone to a different place, a different time and to a new memory. By then, we had grown into two big girls with four large breasts and buttocks like pumpkins and we knew that the stories were not true. Mummy had been to Tanzania – just a boat trip away on Lake Victoria, not London. No Queen Elizabeth.

Mama Atim says you are tired of London. You cannot bear it anymore. London is cold. London is a monster which gives no jobs. London is no cosy exile for the banished. London is no refuge for the immoral. Mama Atim says this word "immoral" to me – slowly and emphatically in Jhapadhola, so it can sink into my head. She wants me to hear the word in every breath, sniff it in every scent so it can haunt me like that day I first touched you. Like the day you first touched me. Mine was a cold unsure hand placed over your right breast. Yours was a cold scared hand, which held my waist and pressed it closer to you, under the jambula tree in front of her house. Mama Atim says you are returning on the wings of a metallic bird – Kenya Airways.

You will land in the hot Kampala heat, which bites at the skin like it has a quarrel with everyone. Your mother does not talk to me or my mother. Mama Atim cooks her kilo of offal which she talks about for one week until the next time she cooks the next kilo again, bending over her charcoal stove, her large and long breasts watching over her saucepan like cow udders in space. When someone passes by, she stops cooking. You can hear her whisper. Perhaps that's the source of her gonorrhoea and Lugogo Show Ground stories. Mama Atim commands the world to her kitchen like her nine sons and one daughter. None of them have amounted to anything. The way their mother talks about me and you, Sanyu, after all these years, you would think her sons are priests. You would think at least one of them got a diploma and a low-paying job at a government ministry. You would think one of them could at least bring home a respectable wife. But *wapi!* their wives are like used bicycles, ridden and exhausted by the entire estate's manhood. They say the monkey which is behind should not laugh at the other monkey's tail. Mama Atim laughs with her teeth out and on display like cowries. She laughs loudest and forgets that she, of all people, has no right to urinate at or lecture the entire estate on the gospel according to St Morality.

Sometimes I wonder how much you have changed. How have you grown? You were much taller than I. Your eyes looked stern, created an air about you – one that made kids stop for a while, unsure if they should trample all over you or take time to see for sure if your eyes would validate their preconceived fears. After they had finally studied, analysed, added, multiplied and subtracted you, they knew you were for real.

When the bigger kids tried to bully me, you stood tall and dared them to lay a finger on me. Just a finger, you said, grinding your teeth like they were aluminium. They knew you did not mince words and that your anger was worse than a teacher's bamboo whipping. Your anger and rage coiled itself like a python around anyone who dared, anyone who challenged. And that's how you fought, with your teeth and hands but mostly with your feet. You coiled them around Juma when he knocked my tooth out for refusing to let him have his way at the water tap when he tried to cheat me out of my turn at the tap.

I wore my deep dark green uniform. At lunch times the lines could be long and boys always jumped the queue. Juma got me just as I put my water container to get some drinking water after lunch. He pushed me away. He was strong Sanyu. One push like that and I fell down. When I got up, I left my tooth on the ground and rose up with only blood on the green; deep green, the colour of the morning when the dew dries off leaves.

You were standing a distance. You were not watching. But it did not take you too long to know what was going on. You pushed your way through the crowd and before the teachers could hear the commotion going on, you had your legs coiled around Juma. I don't know how you do it Sanyu. He could not move.

Juma, passed out? Hahahahahahaha!

I know a lot of pupils who would be pleased with that. Finally his big boy muscles had been crushed, to sand, to earth and to paste.

The thought of that tasted sweet and salty like grasshoppers seasoned with onion and *kamulari* – red, red-hot pepper.

Mr Wangolo came with his hand-on-the-knee-limp and a big bamboo cane. It was yellow and must have been freshly broken off from the mother bamboos just outside the school that morning. He pulled and threatened you with indefinite expulsion before you let big sand-earth-paste Juma go. Both you and Juma got off with a two-week suspension. It was explicitly stated in the school rules that no one should fight. You had broken the rules. But that was the lesser of the rules that you broke. That I broke. That we broke.

Much later, at home, your mother was so angry. On our way home, you had said we should not say how the fight started. We should just say he hit you and you hit him back. Your house was two blocks from ours and the school was the nearest primary school to the estate. Most of the kids in the neighbourhood studied at Nakawa Katale Primary School alright, but everyone knew we were great friends. When your mother came and knocked upon our door, my mother had just put the onions on the charcoal stove to fry the goat's meat.

Mummy bought goat's meat when she had just got her salary. The end of month was always goat's meat and maybe some rice if she was in a good mood. Mummy's food smelt good. When she cooked, she joked about it. Mummy said if Papa had any sense in his head, he would not have left her with three kids to raise on her own to settle for that slut he called a wife. Mummy said Papa's new wife could not cook and that she was young enough to be his daughter. They had to do a caesarean on her when she gave birth to her first son. What did he expect? That those wasp hips could let a baby's head pass through them?

When she talked of Papa, she had that voice. Not a "hate voice" and not a "like voice", but the kind of voice she would use to open the door for him and tell him welcome back even after all these years when he never sent us a single cent to buy food, books, soap or Christmas clothes. My papa is not like your papa, Sanyu. Your papa works at the Ministry of Transport. He manages the Ugandan railways, which is why he wants you to engineer a railway village for him. You say he has gotten so intoxicated with the railways that every time he talks of it, he rubs his palms together like he is thinking of the best ever memory in his life. Your father has a lot of money. Most of the teachers knew him at school. The kids had heard about him. Perhaps that is why your stern and blank expression was interpreted with slight overtones. They viewed you with a mixture of fear and awe; a rich man's child.

Sometimes Mummy spoke about your family with slight ridicule. She said no one with money lived in Nakawa Housing Estates of all places. If your family had so much money, why did you not go to live in Muyenga, Kololo and Kansanga with your Mercedes Benz lot? But you had new shoes every term. You had two new green uniforms every term. Sanyu, your name was never called out aloud by teachers, like the rest of us whose parents had not paid school tuition on time and we had to be sent back home with circulars.

> Dear Parent,
> This is to remind you that unless this term's school fees are paid out in full, you daughter/son … will not be allowed to sit for end of term exams …
> Blah blah blah …

Mummy always got those letters and bit her lip as if she just heard that her house had burnt down. That's when she started staring at the ceiling with her eyes transfixed on one particular spot on the brown tiles.

On such days, she went searching through her old maroon suitcase. It was from another time. It was the kind that was not sold in shops anymore. It had lost its glitter and I wished she never brought it out to dry in the sun. It would be less embarrassing if she brought out the other ones she used for her Tanzania trips. At least those ones looked like the ones your mother brought out to dry in the sun when she did her weekly house cleaning. That suitcase had all Mummy's letters – the ones Papa had written her when, as she said, her breasts were firm like green mangoes. Against a kerosene lamp, she read aloud the letters, reliving every moment, every word and every promise.

> *I will never leave you. You are mine forever. Stars are for the sky, you are for me. Hello my sweet supernatural colours of the rainbow. You are the only bee on my flower. If loving you is a crime I am the biggest criminal in the world.*

Mummy read them out aloud and laughed as she read the words in each piece of stained paper. She had stored them in their original airmail envelopes with the green and blue decorations. Sometimes Papa had written to her in aerogramme. Those were opened with the keenest skill to keep them neat and almost new. He was a prolific letter writer, my papa, with a neat handwriting. I know this because oftentimes I opened her case of memories. I never did get as far as opening any letter to read; it would have been trespassing. It did not feel right, even if Mummy had never scolded me from reading her "To Josephine Athieno Best" letters.

I hated to see her like that. She was now a copy typist at Ramja Securities. Her salary was not much, but she managed to survive on it, somehow, somehow. There were people who spoke of her beauty as if she did not deserve being husbandless. They said with some pity, "Oh, and she has a long ringed neck, her eyes are large and sad. The woman has a voice, soft, kind and patient. How could the man leave her?" Mummy might have been sad sometimes, but she did not deserve any pity. She lived her life like her own fingernails and temperament: so calm, so sober and level-headed, except of course when it came to reading those Papa letters by the lantern lamp.

I told you about all this Sanyu. How I wished she could be always happy, like your mother who went to the market and came back with two large boys carrying her load because she had shopped too much for your papa, for you, for your happy family. I did not tell you, but sometimes I stalked her as she made her way to buy things from the noisy market. She never saw me. There were simply too many people. From a distance, she pointed at things, fruit ripe like they had been waiting to be bought by her all along. Your mother went from market stall to market stall, flashing her white Colgate smile and her dimpled cheeks. Sometimes I wished I were like you; with a mother who bought happiness from the market. She looked like someone who summoned joy at her feet and it fell in salutation, humbly, like the *kabaka* subjects who lay prostate before him.

When I went to your house to do homework, I watched her cook. Her hand stirred groundnut soup. I must admit, Mummy told me never to eat at other people's homes. It would make us appear poor and me rather greedy. I often left your home when the food was just about ready. Your mother said, in her summon-joy-voice: "Supper is ready. Please eat." But I, feigning time-consciousness always said, "I have to run home, Mummy will be worried." At such times, your father sat in the bedroom. He never came out from that room. Everyday, like a ritual, he came home straight from work.

"A perfect husband," Mummy said more times than I can count.

"I hate him," you said more times than I could count. It was not what he didn't do, you said. It was what he did. Those touches, his touches you said. And you could not tell your mother. She would not believe you. She never did.

Like that time she came home after the day you taught Juma a good lesson for messing around with me. She spoke to my mother in her voice which sounded like breaking china.

"She is not telling me everything. How can the boy beat her over nothing? At the school tap? These two must know. That is why I am here. To get to the bottom of this! Right now!"

She said this again and again, and Mummy called me from the kitchen, where I had escaped just when I saw her knock on our back door holding your hands in hers and pulling you behind her like a goat!

"Anyango, Anyangooooo," Mummy called out.

I came out, avoiding your eyes. Standing with my hands held in front of me with the same kind of embarrassment and fear that overwhelmed me each time I heard my name called by a teacher for school fees default.

They talked for hours. I was terrified, which was why I almost told the truth. You started very quickly and repeated the story we had on our way home. Your mother asked, "What was Anyango going to say again?" I repeated what you had just said, and your mother said, "I know they are both lying. I will get to the bottom of this at school in two weeks' time when I report back with her." And she did. You got a flogging that left you unable to sit down on your bum for a week.

When you left our house that day, they talked in low voices. They had sent us outside to be bitten by mosquitoes for a bit. When they called us back in, they said nothing. Your mother held your hand again, goat style. If Juma had seen you being pulled like that, he would have had a laugh one hundred times the size of your trodden-upon confidence. You never looked back. You avoided looking at me for a while after that. Mummy had a list of don'ts after that for me too. They were many. Don't walk back home with Sanyu after school. Don't pass by their home each morning to pick her up. Don't sit next to her in class. Don't borrow her text books. I will buy you your own. Don't even talk to her. Don't, don't, don't do anymore Sanyu.

It was like that, but not for long. After we started to talk again and look each other in the eyes, our parents seemed not to notice, which is why our secondary schools applications went largely unnoticed. If they complained that we had applied to the same schools and in the same order, we did not hear about them.

1. Mary's College Namagunga 2. Nabisunsa Girls' School 3. City High School. 4. Modern High School.

You got admitted to your first choice. I got my third choice. It was during the holidays that we got a chance to see each other again. I told you about my school. That I hated the orange skirts, white shirts, white socks and black boy's Bata shoes. They made us look like flowers on display. The boys wore white trousers, white shorts, white socks, and black shoes. At break time, we trooped like a bunch of moving orange and white flowers – to the school canteens, to the drama room, and to the football field.

You said you loved your school. Sister Cephas your Irish headmistress wanted to turn you all into black English girls. The girls there were the prettiest ever and were allowed to keep their hair long and held back in puffs, not one inch only like at my school.

We were seated under the jambula tree. It had grown so tall. The tree had been there for ages with its unreachable fruit. They said it was there even before the estate houses were constructed. In April the tree carried small purple jambula fruit, which tasted both sweet and tang and turned our tongues purple. Every April morning when the fruit started to fall, the ground became a blanket of purple.

When you came back during that holiday, your cheeks were bulging like you had hidden oranges inside them. Your eyes had grown small and sat like two short slits on your face. And your breasts, the two things you had watched and persuaded to grow during all your years at Nakawa Katale Primary School, were like two large jambulas on your chest. And that feeling that I had, the one that you had, that we had – never said, never spoken – swelled up inside us like fresh *mandazies*. I listened to your voice rise and fall. I envied you. I hated you. I could not wait for the next holidays when I could see you again. When I could dare place my itchy hand onto your two jambulas.

That time would be a night, two holidays later. You were not shocked. Not repelled. It did not occur to either of us, to you or me, that these were boundaries we should not cross nor should think of crossing. Your jambulas and mine. Two plus two jambulas equals four jambulas – even numbers should stand for luck. Was this luck pulling us together? You pulled me to yourself and we rolled on the brown earth that stuck to our hair in all its redness and dustiness. There in front of Mama Atim's house. She shone a torch at us. She had been watching. Steadily like a dog waiting for a bone it knew it would get; it was just a matter of time.

Sanyu, I went for confession the next day, right after Mass. I made the sign of the cross and smelt the fresh burning incense in St Jude's church. I had this sense of floating on air, confused, weak, and exhausted. I told the priest, "Forgive me father for I have sinned. It has been two months since my last confession." And there in my head, two plus two jambulas equals four jambulas …

I was not sorry. But I was sorry when your father with all his money from the railways got you a passport and sent you on the wing of a bird; hello London, here comes Sanyu.

Mama Atim says your plane will land tomorrow. Sanyu, I don't know what you expect to find here, but you will find my mummy; you'll find that every word she types on her typewriter draws and digs deeper the wrinkles on her face. You will find Nakawa Housing Estates. Nothing has changed. The women sit in front of their houses and wait for their husbands to bring them offal. Mama Atim's sons eat her food and bring girls to sleep in her bed. Your mother walks with a stooped back. She has lost the zeal she had for her happiness-buying shopping trips. Your papa returns home every day as soon as he is done with work. My mummy says, "That is a good husband."

I come home every weekend to see Mummy. She has stopped looking inside her maroon case. But I do; I added the letter you wrote me from London. The only one I ever did get from you, five years after you left. You wrote:

A.

I miss you.

S.

Sanyu, I am a nurse at Mengo hospital. I have a small room by the hospital, decorated with two chairs, a table from Katwe, a black and white television and two paintings of two big jambula trees which I got a downtown artist to do for me. These trees have purple leaves. I tell you, they smile.

I do mostly night shifts. I like them, I often see clearer at night. In the night you lift yourself up in my eyes each time, again and again. Sanyu, you rise like the sun and stand tall like the jambula tree in front of Mama Atim's house.

LEAVING CIVVY STREET

ANNIE HOLMES

"Hey, Bev!" my brother Don called out when we got home from school. "Howzit, Elise?" he added when he saw her follow me in the front door. He was out on the verandah with his girlfriend Sherylee curled against him all kittenish. It was camouflage city out there, and a hell of a racket – a bunch of Don's friends drinking beer at Dad's bar, half of them in uniform, the others heading for the Rhodesian Light Infantry in the same intake as my brother the next morning. Same savage haircuts, same strips of untanned neck. From the kitchen I could smell mealie meal and hear the thump of a wooden spoon through a potful of porridge – Cornelius making *sadza* for the braai for Don's last night.

"Come and have a drink with us, man," Don yelled at us. "I'm gonna get donnered tomorrow."

I said, "Ja, okay, just now," and Elise and I headed for my room.

"Don't disappear, you girls," my mom yelled from the kitchen. "Don's last night, remember."

"Okay," we called back and closed the door of my room. Part of me wanted to be out there on a bar stool, laughing with Don and his gang – especially tonight – but Elise unspun my loyalties. Elise charged the air. My eyes had to follow her. Iron filings to the magnet, sunflower to the sun, me to Elise. When she was around, I could hear barely anything else. "By the bang of blood in the brain deaf the ear," like in the Jaguar poem by Ted Hughes.

At school, they called Elise Kalahari, like the desert. Why? Long thin strip of fuck-all. Me they called *kafupi*, half-pint, the blonde dwarf. And the two of us together: Laurel and Hardly. Lanky Elise being Laurel, with me supposedly Hardly There at All. Typical pathetic school humour.

"Do you want to go sit in the bar with everyone?" Elise asked me. "I mean, he's going into the army tomorrow. It's significant."

"We could," I said. I stroked her arm. "He'd like it."

"Yeah, we could."

"For a bit at least."

We unlaced our brown school shoes and peeled off our short white school socks. Elise draw her green school uniform over her head, revealing her pale belly and her purple floral bra as her skinny ribcage reached up. Then she dug in the cupboard for the jeans she kept at my house. I lay on my side on the bed, watching her go through a pile of my T-shirts. Cornelius ironed them so flat, so regimental, that Elise called them slices off a T-shirt loaf.

"Come on, Psycho," she said, as I lay there in my uniform, "are you changing or not?"

"No, Spazz, I'm not changing, I'm constant as the northern star," I said. "I'm true blue."

The front door slammed. "Cornelius!" came my dad's voice. "My suitcase is in the car."

"Coming, Boss!" Cornelius called back.

Elise stood over me on the bed in her knickers and bra, one foot on either side of me, like Colossus or maybe Colossa. She jumped, bouncing me.

From down the passage, my dad yelled for my mom.

"We're out in the bar!" my mom yelled back.

I grabbed Elise's ankles and tumbled her down to the bed. She wriggled around onto her side facing me. Reached out. Ran her hand up my school skirt, between my thighs.

"Bevvy?" called my dad from the passage.

"We'll be out in a second, Dad," I bellowed.

He knocked on the door. "Can I come in?"

"No – we're changing!"

"Well, come out to the bar and say hello."

"Coming!" we chorused. Elise slid her fingers under the elastic of my regulation green cotton knickers. "When you see me looking at this uniform of yours," she said in my ear, "remember this, okay?" I nodded. "Think of my fingers." I swallowed. I touched her wrist to hold her hand there.

"Girls?" said my mom outside the door.

"We're *changing*, Mom!" I yelled indignantly.

"Well, don't take too long, Dad's putting the steak on the braai."

"Okay," we chorused, and then Elise slid her fingers further and I closed my eyes and turned slowly onto my back so I didn't lose her.

Just a few months before, we'd been distant friends in a loose confederacy of classmates, me on the hockey-playing side of things while Elise, on the opposite margins, came to school with a forbidden line of black Indian kajal traced round her eyes. She spoke a secret ironic language with the other freak girls and handed in notes to avoid sport: "Please excuse Elise van der Linde from games this week due to circumstances beyond her control." That was the euphemism for menstruating. "I'm on," we said to each other. "The curse?" mothers asked. "Circumstances," they wrote.

"Very long periods you have," observed the gym teacher, Miss Jenks. "Three weeks of the month, apparently."

Elise looked down at her feet. "Please don't mention it so loudly, ma'am," she said. "It's embarrassing."

Miss Jenks snorted. "You don't look embarrassed to me, Elise," she said.

There I'd be, running with all the other sporty girls, or diving, sprinting, serving and volleying, springing off the trampette and over the horse, while Elise would be talking, talking with the freak girls. When the three of them did actually change into their gym slips and join the PE class, they'd share an exercise mat and sit talking on it until Miss Jenks headed their way, at which point they'd turn as one onto their backs and lift their hips in shoulder stands. "Better than nothing, I suppose," said Miss Jenks and strode on, dimpled jelly legs quivering under her miniscule hockey skirt. A lesbo, for sure, we all said. We'd pull faces at each other if she happened to touch one of us when she helped us leap the horse or straightened our headstand. And we all apologised profusely if we touched each other, in case anyone thought we were "like that". Thursdays were queer days, we said, and what about girls who wore a single earring, or a different sock on each foot, or a different shoe? Lesbos for sure. "Oh God," we said if we saw naïve first form girls holding hands. "Lesbie friends and go homo!"

Gay men, though, that was different. Hairdressers. The TV news reader. That guy at the florist's. Our own classmate Chris, who left school in the middle of form four, everyone knew he was a moffie and, weirdly, even the other boys didn't seem to give him gyp about it. He was at Elise's one Thursday when I went over to work with her on a geography project.

"I can't live here one more day," Chris told us. "Salisbury, Rhodesia? Not me." He was trying on Elise's shoes, plum coloured platforms with ankle straps. Their feet were the same size.

"Maybe I should wear them to the club on Saturday," Chris said.

"Excellent idea, Chris," I said. "Die young." Soldiers would beat a guy up for having hair slightly longer than military style. Never mind wearing girls' platform Mary Janes.

Chris was tempting the school haircut limits, like we did with the skirt lengths of our uniforms ("three inches above the floor when kneeling"). He ran his fingers through what there was of his hair, brown and hinting at curls to come. "I've been reading about Tangiers," he said.

Elise and I exchanged looks. Earth to Chris?

"You're moving to *Durban*," Elise reminded him. Lots of guys left the country right after school to avoid the army, but Chris' family were gapping it early. Just in case.

He flung himself backwards onto Elise's bed, pointing his feet up at the ceiling, admiring the arch of his instep under the ankle strap. "I know," he told Elise, "but Paris calls, you know? London … Milano."

"Can you speak Spanish, Chris?"

"Italian, Beverley. Milano is in Italia."

"I hope he'll be okay," Elise said when Chris left. "He's such a fearless little faggot."

"Moffie."

"Poofta."

"Homo."

"Fairy."

"Fearless Faggot Fairy."

"It's a miracle he hasn't been mashed to a pulp in the toilet somewhere. He puts mascara on before he goes to Club Tomorrow."

"God!"

"And he's such a dreamer. Milano, he says!"

"Tangiers!"

We snorted. But Elise liked him better than all the boys we knew. "Those tedious shit-for-brains," she called them.

"But still, Elise, he, you know …"

"What?"

"You know. He does it with other boys."

"Does it? Does it? Jesus, Bev, how old are you?"

"Okay, he has sex with other boys, with men."

"He fucks them, you mean."

"Or …"

"Or they fuck him. Well, we don't know that, actually. Maybe he only dreams about it."

"Maybe he just wears the shoes."

"Yeah, and maybe he wears girls' underwear. We could ask him."

"But Elise …"

"What?"

"Two boys …"

"So?"

"Well, think about doing it with a girl."

"Use grown-up verbs, Beverley Richards, for godsake."

"Okay, 'screwing' then. If that's what girls do with each other. I mean, euw."

"Well."

"Well what?"

"Think of screwing Mr Driscoll." He was our Maths teacher and that was pretty gross, as a notion to consider. We ran through a whole list – hairy men, chaps with BO, gormless boys, guys with acne, just about every male we knew – screaming louder at each repulsive suggestion.

"So I don't know," Elise said at last, not looking at me. "I think about Mr Driscoll with his pants down and then I compare that with, I don't know, someone beautiful like Stevie Nicks in Fleetwood Mac – it wouldn't be so disgusting to sleep with her."

"Sleep with? Sleep with? How old are *your* verbs, Elise van der Linde?"

We avoided meeting each other's eyes or, God forbid, actually touching each other. But the idea was out there now, prowling. Stevie Nicks, or, you know, some beautiful girl.

Of course, after that we could barely speak to each other at school for weeks. It would've been way too much like an admission of something. I did replay our conversation, though, in my mind, and I'd look at Elise in class, or sitting by the school pool with the freak sisters. I watched her hand holding a pen or the way she settled her basher on the back of her head and it seemed inevitable: one day she would touch me. When would it happen? I didn't know how to wait, but I didn't know how to do anything else either.

Our English teacher made the move for us. He allocated us the same study space, a stock room, a closet really, behind his classroom. Highly prized, a reward for good essay writing. The first day in there, we sat at desks wedged between the shelves, facing *The Knight's Tale* in a set of twenty-four, *For Whom the Bell Tolls*, *A Town Like Alice*, *Troilus and Cressida*. All re-covered in marbled red vinyl by prisoners who'd stamped the titles on the spines in white caps, sometimes skew.

We sat still for a while, model schoolgirls, backs straight, delaying the moment. My hand on my desk, her hand on hers. We moved our innocent hands closer, until our little fingers lay beside each other on the line between the desks: my finger golden brown; hers long and slender, her skin a pale olive that would've tanned if once in a while she'd torn herself out of a book and into the sunshine.

I touched the skin on the top of her hand with one finger. "You're soft, like a dove."

"You've never touched a dove." She was laughing at me.

"But still, I know. Your cells are finer than other people's."

Her eyes went soft when I touched her. We couldn't turn away. She looked at me fiercely. I almost had to laugh because she scared me. Her long brown hair was parted down the middle and tied on either side of her face in bunches, like Pocahontas, and I wanted it loose so I could slip one hand through it, through the silk, and pull. With the other hand I would reach for her breast. I would. I longed to. I did.

Through the bedroom window, we could hear the sound of voices in the garden – my parents, Don and his friends, and my little brother Jeffrey, excited to be hanging out with the big guys. It was night time and I was still in my rumpled school uniform. Elise pulled her jeans on in the dark and then leaned over me. "Beverley Richards, put your clothes on," she whispered in my ear.

Outside, they were gathered round the smoky braai, next to the pool and under the security light, Mom in her deckchair with a brandy and coke. Everyone was listening to Greg. He was older and he'd been in the army for at least a year already. "These guys were *way* out in the bundu, hell and gone," Greg was saying when I went over to kiss my dad and say welcome home. "And they see this bunch of women with pots on their heads walking down this path, okay? Maybe quarter of a kay away."

My mom stopped spraying mozzie repellent on my little brother Jeffrey's ankles to look up at Greg from under her eyebrows. Ready to interrupt him.

"And apparently this one guy had his FN trained on the women and the piccaninnies. The rest of them couldn't figure out why he was so interested in a bunch of women," Greg took a slug of his beer. "Of course, ouens have to watch out, you check. There could be gooks behind those women."

"Greg," said my mom in a warning voice, but he was set on finishing the story.

"And then suddenly," said Greg, "The guy fires! And there's a *moer* of a bloody explosion! Jesus! Those nannies had grenades and bullets and who knows what-all in those pots, man! And this guy knew, don't ask me how, but he knew."

"Did they all die?" came Jeffrey's little-boy voice.

"Slotted, ek sê. One time."

"It's just stories," my mother told Jeffrey. "Don't listen."

"*Nooit*, I swear Mrs Richards," said Greg. "This guy from my platoon told me …"

"Was he there?" Hands on hips, challenging him.

"No, but this other guy told him …"

"I don't want kids listening to this kind of story," my mother said.

Everyone went quiet. Then "Come on, Greg," said Mom. "My glass is empty. Top me up and get yourself another beer."

On the other side of the fire, standing on his own, Don looked to me, suddenly, like a little boy himself. One hand in his pocket, the other gripping the neck of his beer bottle. Barely any hair left on his mown head. Eighteen years old. I tried not to think of him training a rifle on a line of women with pots on their heads. Could Don actually kill someone? Would he? There'd be people trying to kill him, for sure. That song on TV said Rhodesians never die, but soldiers were dying on a regular basis. Farm owners died too, and so did villagers and, apparently, women carrying pots on their heads. Also, missionaries. And people driving in convoys got fired on or blown up. Even passengers on aircraft got shot down from the sky. What was to say your own brother wouldn't drive over a landmine? This was all a terrible mistake. Don should leave, like Chris the moffie had.

My dad was turning meat over the heat. I went over to stand by him. "Dad," I said softly. "I'm scared, Dad. Don might die."

"Don't talk like that, Beverley," he snapped.

He twisted the silver ring my mom had given him a couple of anniversaries ago. It was sleek and aerodynamic, like something you'd mount on the bonnet of a long black car, and it tangled in the sprout of ginger hairs at his knuckle. He took up the braai fork again, speared strings of blistering wors onto a plate and headed inside the house. I followed him into the kitchen, blinking in the bright neon light.

"No, really man, Beverley," he said angrily. "This is your brother you're talking about. Jesus!"

"Okay, okay, I'm sorry."

"Here, Cornelius." Dad dropped the plate of sausages onto the kitchen counter. Cornelius picked it up and covered it with foil. "I just hope nothing does happen to him," Dad said to me in a clenched voice. "I just bloody hope you don't have to look back and remember talking like this." I watched Cornelius slide the plate into the warming drawer. He kept his back to us like he wasn't really listening, like he didn't know all our family secrets. Like he hadn't heard Greg's bush story.

Dad walked out.

Cornelius threw his dishrag over his shoulder. "You help me, Miss Bev," he said. He was getting old now, Cornelius, older even than Dad, with silver threads in his hair. He loaded a tray with paper napkins, chutney, tomato sauce. "Don't spill," he said, putting the tray in my hands.

Outside, Elise and Jeffrey were playing some leaping game on the trampoline, growling and roaring at each other, and that put Sherylee's friend Debbie in mind of a joke. She leaned close to Don's buddy Mark, the good looking one, as I walked by. "What's tall, and growls," Debbie asked Mark, "and fucks like a tiger?" Mark shrugged. "Rrrrowl!" said Debbie, raising faux claws. The guys laughed.

I laid out the paper napkins, twisting them into origami peacocks. Cornelius hurried in and out of the house, silent in his worn white takkies, carrying hamburger buns, mayonnaise, paper serviettes. When all the meat was cooked and the salads served, Elise and I carried our food over to the pool and sat on the diving board, dipping *sadza* and greasy wors into chutney. Stu came and stood over us, beer-bold. "So Bev," he said, "Wanna go to the movies with me sometime?" Everyone made fun of Stu, the runt of Don's gang, so Elise and I stuck up for him sometimes, but in the condescending way of princesses. No reason for him to get drunk and stupid about me, though. "Go away, Stu."

"Ag, come on, Bev man, you're a big girl now." Stu made a move to sit between us on the sandpaper surface of the diving board, but we leaned our shoulders in to block him. "You can't stick around with Elise all the time," he said. "You need a boyfriend."

"And you think you're my only option, hey Stu?"

Held in the vee of my brother's arm, Sherylee was listening. Now, she reached over and smacked Stu across the arm with a long metal braai fork. "Leave Bev alone, Stu," she ordered.

"Dammit, Sherylee! You've put grease all over my clothes, man!"

"Don't swear at my girlfriend, Stu," said Don. "Anyone bloody swears at Sherylee, it should be me." Everyone laughed. Sherylee pouting, kissing my brother. The night before the army, the last night on civvy street. Frogs were starting up in the vlei, rawk rawk, and crickets too. Bugs zinged up against the security light.

My dad came over and patted my shoulder. "Okay, my girl," he said quietly, as the rest of them headed back into the bar.

"I'm sorry, Dad," I said.

"It's okay, Bevvy," he said. "It's okay."

Elise and I stayed outside on the diving board above the glow of the swimming pool. Elise hugged her knees, her long back rounded like the letter C. Most nights, I'd do anything for a chance like this to hold her hand secretly and say lines from our favourite poems, "Glory be to God for dappled things," like the lace shadows of the msasa trees on the swimming pool and because we loved "All things counter, original, spare, strange." But tonight, I wanted to curl into my family, like Sherylee curled into my brother's side.

We heard a crash, something breaking in the bar. A girl screamed – Sherylee or Debbie – and then everyone laughed. "Cornelius!" my mom yelled, and he came from the kitchen with a brush and dustpan.

"Let's go and live in Denmark when we finish school," Elise said. "There's no war there. And we could get married."

I tried to picture Denmark, "the breakfast nation of Europe," our geography teacher had told us, "Lots of dairy products, and pig farming for bacon." Would my cousins wear turquoise satin bridesmaids' dresses at our wedding, mine and Elise's, in the breakfast nation of Europe?

"What about your mother?" I asked Elise. "Wouldn't she just die if we went to Denmark and got married?"

"We wouldn't tell her. We wouldn't tell anyone."

We'd have to steal away, anonymously, and never be heard of again. I felt our Danish loneliness in advance.

"Beverley?" called my mom from the bar.

"My mom wants me."

"Well, go then."

"Come with me."

"I'll come just now."

Elise had asked me to marry her, kind of, and I'd said nothing. It made me feel ill to think about it. Denmark. No return.

"Here she is!" Dad said when I walked into the bar. "Come and be sociable, Bevvy." Jeffrey had gone to bed and the rest of them were all drunk now or getting there. Stu climbed off his bar stool so I could sit next to my brother.

"You guys are plastered!" I told them and everyone roared like I was wit personified.

Cornelius came through from the kitchen with the big yellow plastic salt shaker and a bowl of lemon slices. "We going to down swizzingers, Bevvy," Sherylee told me. "Like you do with tequila, only with vodka instead. Say 'swizzinger' Stu."

"Schwizh, schwizhinzher." Stu's head jerked abruptly as he slurred. He didn't look like he'd be lasting long.

"No stamina, boet," said Mark, shaking his head. Debbie leaned up against Mark's stool but he ignored her.

Sherylee demonstrated a swizzinger. First, she made a fist, and licked the skin between her thumb and index finger so salt would stick there. Then, in quick succession, she knocked back a tot of chilled vodka, licked the salt from her fist and sucked on a lemon slice. A vehement shiver ran through her and she arched her neck like a horse, looking up at my brother from under her eyelashes. "Ooh baby," she purred and everyone applauded.

Then the whole gang started licking and salting their fists, reaching for the lemons, my dad sloshing vodka into tot glasses with golfing motifs. I was watching Don to see how he did it, but Mark got off his bar stool, abandoning Debbie, and stood behind me. "Like this, Bevvy," he said in my ear, putting both arms around me. The prickle of his shaved cheek rubbed against my cheek. This is a boy, I thought. This is not Denmark. Mark lifted my fist and licked the spot, slowly. My mother was watching and pretending not to watch and smiling a little to herself. The bar went quiet. Mark was the smoothie, the ladies' man. Him holding me like this was tribal, his friend-of-the-family duty. Don's mates thought I was boring and also a bit scary. Bevvy, the smart one with the weird friends, who reads a lot of books.

I leaned back against Mark and looked round the table. Everyone was watching. I threw back the vodka, licked the salt, sucked on the lemon and felt the same tremble ripple me. Mark nuzzled against my neck for a second and then tossed back his own tot. My dad refilled the glasses. Stu reached for one but Don stopped him. Greg put an LP on the stereo. *They'd been through the desert on a horse with no name. It felt good to be out of the rain.* I made myself forget about Elise on the diving board. I couldn't work out how to keep her in my mind at the same time as I felt Mark's tongue on my fist. There was no pause in Mark, no question. It was simple to lean back against him.

"That's enough for you, young lady," Mom said after my third or fourth swizzinger.

Mark ran his finger down my neck and then took his arms away, moving over to Debbie. My back was cold where he'd been behind me. Air was all around me and a kind of shame. I climbed off the stool and made myself walk slowly out of the bar and outside to find Elise, but she'd gone. No running, I told myself, as if I were a prefect on corridor duty.

She was in my bedroom. "I'm going home," she said. "I'm calling my mom to come and get me." She shook me off and I followed her to the telephone table by the front door.

"Elise," I said, keeping my panicked voice low. "Don't go. You hate your house."

"Not as much as I hate this house." She pushed my hand off the phone and glared at me, cold.

"Oh, don't go," I whispered, the sting of vodka and lemon on my tongue. "I'm so sorry. I'm sorry I'm sorry I'm sorry."

I was. I could see her swallowing. I knew that her heart wanted to crack in her throat, just like mine did. I didn't understand how I could do this to her.

Stu came up, still more or less on his feet. "Bev," he said in the flat voice of the super-drunk.

"Bugger off, Stu," I said.

"Uh, come on, Bev," he said. He staggered and put a hand on the wall to steady himself. "You two," he said, some suspicion dawning in him, "you two girls ..."

"Stu, you're pissed," I said. "You won't even remember this tomorrow." Elise pushed past him and I followed her back to my bedroom. I was going to lock Stu out and Elise in, but before I closed my door, Don came down the passage. My big brother, on his last night on civvy street. Distracted, drunk, not seeing Stu or me at all.

Cornelius heard him and looked out from the kitchen. He was wiping his hands on his apron. "Good night, Boss," he said. "I'm going off now."

"Okay," said Don. "Thanks hey, Cornelius."

Cornelius stood there a moment longer, watching Don sway. Don shook his head. "It's okay, Cornelius. I'm fine," he said. He didn't look fine.

"Okay, Boss," said Cornelius. He went back into the kitchen and closed the door.

ASKING FOR IT

NATASHA DISTILLER

Julia sat in the waiting room, waiting. The carpets were a depressing green, slightly dingy, although the walls were bright and covered with hundreds of colourful images. Julia's mouth was dry and her blood sang in her ears, the by-now familiar sensations of fear and anticipation: adrenalin. She ran her left hand along her right arm, twisting her own flesh to better see the intricate Celtic knot that entwined itself around her bicep. She shifted her weight, and the fifty rand notes in her jeans pocket rustled softly against each other. She sighed, glanced at the decorated walls once more, and smoothed the piece of paper resting on her knee. Looking at the image it bore, she traced yet again the graceful curves of its lines, seeing with satisfaction how they twined together to form a woman's body coalescing out of smoke that snaked from an intricately decorated Aladdin's lamp. She pictured the image rippling slightly with the movement of her upper thigh, as it would when she moved, as it would when she wrapped her legs around Cath. Cath. Cath would like it, for sure. Cath would stroke it, stroke her, and smile her slow smile, and laugh low in the back of her throat. Sitting in the waiting room of the tattoo parlour, Julia felt a rush of warmth, and the fear and anticipation disappeared behind the longing.

The first time they had touched each other, Cath had run her strong hand along the small dolphin that curved its way just underneath Julia's collarbone.

"I know it's a bit corny," Julia had said, embarrassed by the close scrutiny, "but I really like dolphins. They're so … free, you know?"

Cath had only leant forward, and very gently kissed the dolphin, and then kissed Julia. That had been their second date. When they had sex for the first time, Cath had initiated it by slowly tracing the curve of the dolphin with one long finger, and then repeating its shape lower and lower, until she traced a dolphin around Julia's nipple, which she coloured in with her warm, warm tongue.

After they had been together for a few weeks, Cath had said, "You know, I really like your tat."

Julia had smiled, and said, "I know, Cath."

After they had been together a few months, Cath had examined the small dolphin carved into Julia's flesh so many times that Julia was sure she knew every stipple, every slight variation in shade, every tiny follicle in the skin around the tattoo. Certainly, the nerves in Julia's breast were attuned to the tingle of Cath's breath as she gazed at the dolphin; were familiar with the beautiful pressure of the ends of Cath's fingers; would reach, aching, for Cath's lips as they slowly enclosed the dolphin, the bone above the dolphin, the burning flesh below it. Julia loved the way Cath examined her dolphin. Julia loved Cath.

For their three-month anniversary, Julia went to have another tattoo, to surprise Cath. She sat in the slightly dingy green foyer, trembling with excitement, thinking only of Cath's reaction to the scene of cascading water and the mermaid that would now frame and interact with the beloved, loving dolphin. She was so busy thinking of Cath's reaction, and the hours of slow bliss that would follow, that she entirely forgot about the pain. She was startled back into the reality of her present body, and out of the dream of her body as it would feel with Cath, by the biting pain of the needle and its electric whine. She almost jumped with shock and dismay, and only just stopped herself in time; imagine if she caused the tattooist to slip, to jab a sharp black line through the precious dolphin! She lay there, biting her lip but quiet for the rest of the time, as he laid the extended pattern of her love into the soft skin of her upper torso. When Cath saw it that night, the skin still raw and slightly inflamed, but not yet scabbing over, her eyes shone, and she monitored the healing of the image each day with her hands, lips, eyes. Julia was so happy. Whenever she got out of the shower, or changed her shirt, she would look at the aquatic scene that fell along her left breast, and smile.

Seven months later, their relationship hit a rough patch. Julia couldn't understand what was going on in Cath's head, and Cath couldn't, or wouldn't tell her. They would go to bed at night, tight, strained, and dry, and wake up unhappy. Then they tried to talk but invariably they ended up shouting. Eventually, Cath moved out, and Julia sat desolate with grief for a hellish fortnight. When Cath came back, able to talk now, Julia cried hot wet tears of relief and, to celebrate Cath's return, they picked out a design of a baroque Cupid, to lie horizontally across Julia's back, one arm extended and grasping his notched bow, with the arrow pointing diagonally towards her right shoulder. It was by far the bigger of the two tattoos, and Julia liked it. It was, as Cath said, a bit kitsch but still beautiful, like true love. It took three and a half hours to do, the electric needle singing its magic song, and Julia found that she enjoyed the pain a little, when the tattooist didn't leave the point in her skin for too many seconds at a time. After the tattoo came hours of back massages with Julia lying on her stomach while Cath examined the picture on her back, and then turned her over.

When they'd been together almost fourteen months, Julia began to notice that Cath hardly ever looked at the first design anymore. She knew the dolphin, and the mermaid, and the curling patterns of the water so well, she said, that she didn't have to see them; she could picture them in perfect detail in the darkness of her closed lids. A few weeks later, on impulse, Julia popped into a new tattoo parlour that had opened up in Sea Point. The designs were standard, but the photographs of the tattooist's completed works looked good and, because she had extra money in her purse (she had been on her way to do the monthly shopping), she impulsively chose a pixie sitting perched on a large toadstool, a mischievous expression on its face, and told the tattooist to inscribe it on her calf, just above her ankle. That tattoo was the cause of much mirth for Cath, because whenever Julia wore shorts and sandals, people would glance sidelong at her feet. Once, when they were out for brunch on a Sunday morning, sitting at Café Paradiso with the early April sunshine still hot enough to warrant bare legs, a little girl had approached Julia, wondering, and had been allowed a closer look. Her mother had stood at a distance, smiling apologetically, as the child asked what the fairy's name was. As soon as they had left, Cath had grabbed Julia's face in her hands and kissed her hard, and long, and had said, "Let's go home right now." They had left money on the table, not even waiting for the bill to be brought, and had run, hand in hand and laughing, to the car.

Julia remembered the feeling of Cath's hand in hers as they drove home that morning, Cath changing gears with her right hand so as not to have to let go of Julia. They had spent the rest of the day naked in the lounge, with the stereo, a large packet of Pretzolas, and each other.

Julia sighed, and stretched her legs in front of her as she sat in the green waiting room. She tended to prefer this tattooist, the one around the corner from Greenmarket Square. He had added to the aquatic design on her left breast and shoulder, and had inked a cascade of shooting stars and swirling night down her corresponding right side. Across her belly ran a garden scene, with a white unicorn amongst trees and flowers. Cath had said she really liked the unicorn, because it was a symbol of beauty. She had stroked the unicorn many times, which Julia loved because it was on her lower tummy, which was particularly sensitive and mildly ticklish, and could turn quickly to aching desire. After that, when Cath no longer needed to gaze on the magic garden, Julia had the zodiac circle done around her Cupid – interlocking black lines that had taken hours to do. That had been in Brazil, though, in a brightly sterilised room, when Julia and Cath had been on holiday. They had saved for the tattoo before they'd gone, hearing from a friend who had lived there about this particular tattooist. Next had been the Celtic ropes spiralling along each arm, first the left and then the right, a few weeks later, because Cath loved the look of the black ink on Julia's skin. The pixie on her calf had been joined by three others, travelling up her leg on their little toadstools. Now, on her other leg, she would start her genie collection.

The woman, dressed all in black – she was only ever dressed in black, whenever Julia saw her, whether it was at work in the tattoo parlour or hanging out at the Square – came out of the room beyond the archway Julia knew so well by now.

"Okay, Julie, he's nearly ready for you," she said. She had always called Julia "Julie", having got it wrong the first time Julia had booked for her waterscape.

"Thanks," Julia said.

"Coffee?" the woman asked her. Julia had never found out her name, despite her regular appearances at the tattoo parlour over the last couple of years. They had shared cigarettes, and pleasantries, but never her name.

"Ah, no thanks," Julia replied, smiling She was anticipating the needle now, and everything it had grown to represent – the initial pain, and the pleasure that would inevitably follow. The way she would sweat while she was on the chair that looked almost exactly like a dentist's, the weight of the tattooist's body leaning against hers as he concentrated on his work. The way time would stretch and warp, so that hours condensed or expanded to the rhythm of the heavy metal that he always played on a miniature hi-fi system. He hardly ever spoke to her. His name was Grant.

"Okay." Goth flashed a smile and disappeared through a door opposite the archway, which Julia knew led to the small toilet, sink and kettle. Julia reached into her jacket pocket and took out her cigarettes, but as she was about to light one, a young woman of about twenty came out of the archway, a big patch of white tissue stuck to her arm with surgical tape.

"So, three hours and then I wash it?" she asked over her shoulder. Grant followed her out into the green room.

"Three to four," he said. "See how it's feeling. And not too wet – just to get the Vaseline off."

The young woman nodded. Goth came out of the kitchen, with a mug in her hand. She put her coffee down on the book that was spread across the desk next to the archway. Julia watched the round coffee stain seep into the paper.

"Okay?" Goth asked the young woman, who nodded, put her hand across her tissue bandage and smiled.

Grant turned to Julia and said, "Come," and as she left the room Goth was saying, "So, that'll be two hundred rand."

"Hi," Grant said, as he sat on his stool next to the long chair. "What're we doing?"

Julia showed him the image, smoothing the paper onto the arm of the chair. This," she said, "but can you make her eyes green? And can you get that smoky quality? And I want her hair longer, not so curly."

He took the picture from the chair and scrutinised it. "Mm. Okay. Fine," he said. "Obviously, it won't look exactly like this – the texture I mean, but you should have a pretty good idea of how it will turn out."

"Ja." Julia trusted him. She knew his work.

"Let me just draw it up," he said. He pulled the stool over to a low desk, which was cluttered with inks, bits of paper and tissue, and a roll of tracing paper. Julia settled herself into the chair to wait.

Unrolling the thin white paper, he covered the picture Julia had brought, and bent over it. Julia watched the muscles in his back twitch as he moved, his vest exposing his arms and shoulders, as well as the myriad images inscribed on his upper body. He put his whole body into his work, she thought. The pencil skritched over the tracing paper, as he leaned into the drawing, sketching with large swoops of his arm. About ten minutes later, he straightened and turned to face her.

"Alright?" he asked, as he held up the tracing.

She took it from him; it was almost exactly like the picture she had given him. "Cool, but can you make her hair not so curly?"

"Yep." He took the flimsy paper back and, with an eraser in one hand and the pencil in the other, straightened the genie's curly hair. "That okay?"

Julia nodded. "Great," she said.

"Alright. Where're we putting it?"

"On my right thigh," Julia said. She kicked off her boots and undid her jeans, feeling, as she always did, a little awkward to be taking off her clothes in front of this stranger. He turned away and busied himself with the inks.

"What colours are we using?" he asked, with his back to her.

"Um … I thought quite a lot of grey for the smoke, and maybe green and purple for the lamp, and green in her eyes. What do you think?"

He looked at the image. "*Ja*. I don't think you want to put too many colours in there, especially since you want to get that wispy effect. I can do green and purple. Maybe a little orange too, to make the lamp brighter. It'll contrast well with the smoke. Red lips?"

"No, I thought she should be all grey, except the eyes." Julia had an image of how the genie would look, insubstantial and mysterious, with her knowing green eyes standing out against the smoke.

"Okay." He took a handful of little plastic caps from a paper box, and squirted ink from plastic tubes carefully into each cap. White, black, orange, two different greens, one more turquoise than the other, purple. "Yo!" he yelled. "Bring me a cup of water." Then he pulled two latex gloves out of a drawer, and put them on. From another paper box he took out a needle. "Sealed," he said to her, as he peeled off the paper. She nodded. This was standard procedure; he showed her the new needle each time. He picked up the silver casing, examining it closely, and then slipped in the needle, snapping the elastic that fitted around its back with a quick, practised movement. He checked that it was plugged in, and gave it an experimental buzz. Goth came in with a plastic cup half-filled with water.

"Thanks, babe," he said, and Julia wondered, not for the first time, if they were lovers.

"'kay," Goth said, smiled at Julia, and left.

Grant selected a CD from a haphazard pile under the desk, shoved it into his small hi-fi, which was also under the desk, and pushed play. Speakers on either side of Julia's chair came alive, as the thump and grind of Metallica's Justice for All began. He turned to face her, holding the tracing and a small stick of roll-on deodorant.

"Here," Julia said, turning slightly on her side and showing him her upper thigh. He positioned the image, which took up most of her thigh across, and reached about halfway down.

"Okay?"

Julia shifted the tracing slightly. "There," she said.

He nodded, half to her and half in time to the music, and rubbed her thigh with deodorant. It felt cool on her skin. Then he quickly laid the tracing over the stickiness of the wet deodorant, and rubbed it with the heel of his hand, hard. Peeling off the tracing paper, he showed Julia the image, which now looked clumsy, thick-lined and back to front, on her body.

"Fine," she said.

He threw the tracing paper onto the desk, picked up the needle, buzzed it once, dipped it in the water and then in the black ink. Julia tensed as he leaned over her, and he twisted his body so that his elbow was leaning on her thigh. It was an impersonal contact, professional and necessary, and he was heavy. The needle whined over the music, and Julia's skin awaited its first bite.

The tattoo took almost two hours, shorter than Julia had expected, probably because the smoke-effect required less detail than the rest of the image, and composed about half of the overall picture. When Grant was finished, he stretched his arms across his chest, wiped her aching skin once more with the piece of bloody tissue he was holding in his gloved hand, then smeared her new tattoo with Vaseline and covered it with a clean square of tissue. Julia knew that the tissue would be stained and crusty when she peeled it off. He pulled off the gloves and stood.

Julia's body felt twisted and cramped, sore from lying in one position, sore from the weight of his elbow digging into her, sore and red and bruised from the needle. But she felt elated. The tattoo was really beautiful, striking and effective. She knew Cath would like it, could anticipate the feel of Cath's gaze on her thigh as she pored over the new image. She paid and left, shivering slightly as the setting sun died over the street and the wind blew chill from the sea.

When she got home, Cath was reading on the couch. "Hey. How's it look?"

"Good. Great." Julia peeled off the tissue, careful not to tear it, and showed Cath.

"It's gorgeous, Gorgeous!" Cath said, and smiled at her quickly before turning her eyes back to the magazine she was paging through.

Julia put the tissue back in place, pushing the surgical tape to make it re-stick.

"You don't like it?" she asked, feeling a thin line of fear screech across the inside of her belly, like a needle, like a knife. Cath looked up again, too quickly, and her eyebrows were pinched together. Julia heard her voice through the pounding of blood in her ears.

"I said it's lovely, Jule, very nice. Okay? Now, do you mind? I'm trying to read."

THE BIG STICK

RICHARD DE NOOY

How much anger and despair did you choke down, Princess, on your way to the station? But still you stood and waved nicely until Ma had crossed the bridge and disappeared into town. Only then did you seek refuge behind a tree to throw up your farewell brunch in three long hurls. Then you cried and cried until you could cry no more. She had kept it short – a quick hug, a peck on the cheek and then the words that echoed hollow through your head: "Don't cry now. It's for your own good. Follow your heart."

Bullshit. Your heart had always deceived you, as she bloody well knew. That's why you had to leave. She could have waited till the train came. She could have stood on the platform waving you off with her white hanky. But she didn't. She was like the wily jackal that gathers wool in its mouth and then backs slowly into the river until all the fleas have fled into the fluff. Then it drops the wool and takes off like a flash, outwitting the fleas. You were the wool, Princess, floating on the river, the memories like vermin on your skin. Your entire body itched.

You dragged your big brown suitcase up the stairs and stood sweating in the sun. You chased the itch from your lower leg to your upper arm, then through your hair and down your spine, where it hid under the little rucksack with valuables strapped tight against your back. The rucksack contained:

A fresh Dutch passport
A one-way train ticket to Johannesburg
A one-way plane ticket to Amsterdam
A tattered textbook titled *Zoo Spreekt Men Nederlandsch*
A Rubik's Cube with one side done (orange)
And a transparent plastic raincoat, tightly folded into a nifty bag.

That last item was utterly useless on the platform in Zeerust. God had come to see you off personally, Princess, to make sure you got on that train. His breath like a bellows across the parched tracks. The dusty embers scorching your face and arms, giving you a taste of hell to come.

You sought the shelter of a pillar. Your shoulders hunched like useless wings under the pale blue cotton of your shirt. But the wind kept turning you like a chicken on an upright spit, spiked through the jacksie, the rod driving your pants into your damp crotch.

The suit was Ma's farewell gift. She had driven you all the way to Rustenburg to buy it. At Barry's Men's Wear. You went in the Merc, which Solly had washed and polished the day before. Ma was in full regalia: white cotton skirt, white blouse with lace trimmings, dark blue blazer with bright copper buttons, tan stockings and her dark blue Daisy Duck pumps. The car reeked of Charlie, the elixir of youth, five-ninety-five a flacon. It was on your tongue, up your nose, in your brain, never to be forgotten. You cracked the window. Speed became sound. You were howling along at one hundred and forty decibels per hour. Ma made a tired, up-up gesture with her hand, and you fooped the window shut.

You drove on in silence. Your whole life, all the unsaid shit, riding along on the roof. You just had to reach up and grab a fistful – it would have given you enough to talk about till Rustenburg, till Joburg, till Cairo even. But the window stayed firmly shut.

Barry had been your mother's last test. He greeted you and Ma as if you were long lost friends. His whole body was very, very happy, as if every word brought to mind a song. His shop was his stage. And he put on a great show. Every time you went to change your pants, Barry thrust his head through the curtains and bellowed: "Not too tight around the derrière?"

Most boys were scared of beaming Barry. But not you, Princess. It was as if someone was whistling your song. You wanted to sing along. You couldn't stop smiling. Your cheeks ached. And Barry kept going – cracking jokes, swopping winks, flouncing curtains.

Ma was a lone spectator. Her mouth set in a gentle smile, her eyes sad. Like a judge listening to a child's testimony. She knew the truth, Princess, but she wanted to know if the truth would make you happy. She got all the proof she needed when you stepped out for the fifth time, wearing the full three-piece rig. Barry flopped down into his leather armchair, clapped his hand over his mouth, and whispered: "You were born to wear that suit."

When Ma saw you beaming, proud as a peacock, with eyes only for Barry, she knew enough. Not long thereafter you were told you would be leaving. She had made all the arrangements.

You were thirsty, Princess, but you didn't dare go into the café. You had seen the wolves sitting there when you arrived. Their brown uniforms told you they were from the hunting ground, that place of pain and camaraderie where they had cut their white fangs, wrestling in the sun, laughing and howling in the moonlight, taking communal showers. You had tried to understand their world, Princess, but their lair remained a labyrinth where danger lurked in every corner.

Some say fear clutches the heart like a cold fist. But that's bullshit. Fear is warm and bright and courses through every fibre, neuron and corpuscle. Every single cell is built to survive. And fear is the fluid that conveys the rallying call. Fear had been your guiding light as you stumbled through the darkness in search of an exit. It was fear that led you to The Big Stick.

You found it on the floor of the changing room, rolled up in a tight ball, naked, shattered, as Bok's wrath rained down on you. You had learned not to look, hard lessons delivered by fist and flat hand. You could keep your head down for ages as you buffed your toes or dried your hair – the towel like a damp curtain shielding you from things you should not see. But Bok, the alpha male, had howled as he whipped some poor bugger with his wet towel, and you had looked up, straight into his hairy basket where his one-eyed cobra swayed to and fro.

Danie Maritz was looking too. But when he saw that you had seen him clocking Bok's cock, he shouted: "Hey, Bok! This *moffie* wants a piece of your package!"

You blushed and said no-no-no, but Bok was already on his way over with his towel. The wet whip stung five, six, seven times, as you tried to get away, tripping. Then Bok planted his foot in your gut and said between his teeth: "This cock belongs to Bok! And if you even think of looking at it again, I will fuck you up so bad, you'll wish you'd never been born!"

That was when you found The Big Stick. Right there and then, curled up on the cold floor, you began thinking about Bok's cock. And you didn't just think about looking at it. You thought about all the other things you'd like to do with it. And you thought about Bok thanking you for doing those things. And you thought about the other guys watching as you and Bok thanked each other.

Bok saw The Big Stick rising in your groin and stepped back a pace. You tried to hide it, scrambling for your towel, but everyone had seen it. And although they laughed uneasily and sissed in disgust, they backed off. The mere suspicion that fear and pain might be experienced as pleasure was enough to brand you a leper. And so you spent your last two years at school in quarantine, Princess. Free of persecution, but desperately alone, plagued by bestial fantasies.

Cast out from your herd, you stood at the station. The wolves inside the café knew nothing of The Big Stick. They saw only a strange, sick creature in a tight-fitting suit, just begging to be mauled and eaten. And so you chose to stay outside, hiding behind a pillar at the far end of the platform. Afraid to go and take a piss. Afraid to go inside and buy a Coke. Afraid to walk or speak out loud, knowing that you would stand out like a pink dress in a coal mine.

The miners would first gawk at the garment, caught in the light of their helmet lamps. They would laugh and point and crack jokes. Then the boldest or simplest soul would plant his blackened boot on the dress, and they would laugh some more. Then the joker would slip it on for a rip-roaring girlie imitation. This would get his mates all hot and bothered. They would grab him and drape him over a trolley, lift up his dress, tear open his overalls, and one by one …

The wolves were coming out – growling, barking, howling. The train was coming. You would wait until they were all aboard before leaving the shelter of the pillar. Ma's golden rules echoed through your head: Be elegant, but don't walk like Gina Lollobrigida; Sing in private, but whistle in public; Keep it short and simple, don't enthuse; Be proud of who you are, but don't tell people what you are.

But nobody was fooled, Princess. You couldn't hide it. They had all tried to bend you straight – Ma, Elana, Boet and Frik, Oom Andries and many others – but none of them had succeeded. It was there for all to see. Even the porter who stowed your big brown suitcase spotted it straight away, even though there probably wasn't a word in his language to describe your condition.

SETHUNYA LIKES GIRLS BETTER

WAME MOLEFHE

It was the headline that caught her eye:

> **Ape on the Run Shot Dead**
>
> Johnnie, a forty-one-yearold chimpanzee, was shot dead by staff after he escaped from his enclosure … Hundreds of visitors were told to lock themselves in their cars. The drama unfolded in the morning, soon after the zoo opened … An employee described Johnnie as a "bit of a thug".
>
> When asked why Johnnie was killed, the warden gave the following statement: "An informed decision was taken to shoot the chimpanzee. Management believed that Johnnie presented a very real threat to the human population. Investigations have commenced to establish the cause of the chimpanzee's escape. We are all grieving for Johnnie."

Sethunya pictured the scene at the zoo: cars filling the parking lot, buses offloading camera-carrying tourists, children laughing, and the clamour of foreign tongues as sightseers jostled for seats in the Land Rovers waiting to take them to the man-made lake. The air at the top of the hill would have made her feel like she was closer to heaven and, down below, troops of monkeys were scampering through bush. Farther away, impala and duiker leapt across the grass.

Visitors followed a gravel path from the lake to the animal enclosures, parents holding tight to their children's hands to keep them at a respectful distance from the wild creatures. They gathered around the chimpanzees' cage, and listened as the guide pointed out Johnnie and his mate. Cameras flashed. A boy broke away from the rest and faced up to Johnnie, pounding his fists against his chest and grunting, until his mother dragged him back with an angry slap and the group moved on.

Then Johnnie escaped.

Sethunya thought of how she had fled her mother's home to become Thato's wife. Thato was a good man, kind and gentle, and when Father Simon said, "You may kiss your bride," when Thato lifted her veil and looked into Sethunya's eyes, she knew he loved her and that his love would put to rest those other thoughts she sometimes had.

After the church ceremony, she had returned to the home she had grown up in for the last time. She stepped out of stilettos into flat sandals, and exchanged the white silk gown for a traditional *leteisi* to wait with her mother for her relatives, who would deliver her to her in-laws.

"Sethunya, you must wear something on your head."

She had watched her mother search in her chest of drawers for a scarf with which to cover her hair. She watched her rummaging around in her sewing box for a pin to secure a shawl across her shoulders. She felt her sigh as she pinned the brooch on.

"Please listen to what the women tell you, my child," her mother had said. "They know what marriage is."

"Don't worry, Mma. I won't embarrass you."

Her mother did not respond.

"Mma, why aren't you coming?"

"It's not allowed."

"Why not?"

But Sethunya knew, even before her mother had said the words.

"This is how things are done."

Sethunya's aunt had arrived to fetch her niece then, and they stood together outside her mother's home, three good Batswana women, watching as the trunk her mother had packed was hauled onto the back of a van. It had taken four muscled men to lift it. Her mother had filled it to bursting with pretty new bed linen, ordered from her special catalogue: down pillows, snow-white sheets with pretty flowers, an embroidered eiderdown, and blankets. When it was time for her to leave, Sethunya held her mother's hand.

"Trust in God," her mother said, "and everything will be fine."

Tied to the front gate of her in-laws' home, a triangular white cloth had waved in the breeze, announcing that there would be a wedding and everyone was welcome. By the verandah, little girls sang, "Monyadi wa rona. O tshwana le naledi." Our bride looks as lovely as a star. As Sethunya approached the house, men and women rushed to claim her, and she was swept into the throng of swirling skirts and stomping feet. When the joyous reception lulled, the men and young girls resumed their roles, leaving the married women to complete the last marriage ritual.

Sethunya had sat village-style, with her legs tucked under her, on a goat skin, looking up at the women who encircled her. They reminded her of her mother: the same age, the same wraparound *mateisi* and plaited hair hidden under doeks, the same conviction that marriage was a good woman's trophy.

She had not known what to expect; only what she had gleaned from conversations whispered by girls who knew no more than she

– that married women were going to tell her what society expected of a good Motswana wife.

Her nervousness had played out in the way she toyed with her wedding ring, twisting it round and round and then pulling it off and slipping it back on again. A woman sitting behind her tapped her shoulder and whispered into her ear, "Ga e rolwe."

Sethunya had slipped her hands beneath her thighs and smiled. Yes, she would get used to her wedding ring and, like the woman had said, she would never take it off.

Her father's sister had spoken first.

"When a woman marries, her life changes; she must leave behind unmarried friends."

"A wife does not ask her husband where he has been when he comes home."

"A woman must cook for her husband," said another aunt.

"Bear him a son."

"Care for his parents."

"Do not discuss your marriage with others."

"Pray."

Sethunya wanted to ask who made these rules. But she knew the answer. This is how things are done.

Then her mother-in-law had stood up and undone the doek that Sethunya wore on her head, replacing it with one she took out of her bag. She picked up a jug of water and an empty glass and began to pour the water into the glass. The glass overflowed and water spilt onto the sand, but she kept pouring until the jug was empty.

"You're my daughter now and my heart overflows with love for you," she said.

As Sethunya had stood up, she felt tears sting her eyes. She wiped them away as she stood up to hug her new mother. Yes, this was how things were meant to be. No one could then say she liked girls better.

Sethunya imagined Johnnie hurtling over picnic tables, chasing freedom, chasing the sun, frightening old men as they hobbled across the park hand in hand with their grandchildren.

The game warden, in his worn leather sandals and white socks, rifle in hand, charged after Johnnie. She heard the first bullet rip through Johnnie's skull, felt the second go through his heart, and she saw Johnnie running, slower and slower, as if in a movie in slow-motion replay, till he crumpled to the ground in front of the sign with chipped paint that said DON'T FEED THE ANIMALS. Blood pooling around his coal-black head, Johnnie died with his eyes open.

"What's wrong?" Thato whispered. He moved closer to Sethunya, rousing her from her daydream, but she was still at the zoo, wondering why the zookeeper hadn't warned Johnnie first. He could have fired a bullet into the air, or maybe tranquillised him like they did on wildlife programmes.

She shook her head, wondering if the bullet that went through Johnnie's heart had pierced his soul. She wondered if animals had souls. She knew God gave people souls and their souls went to heaven when they died – if they'd been good on earth. She remembered Noah's ark and how the animals went in two by two. God saved the animals from the terrible floods so he must have given them souls too, like people. She prayed her soul would go to heaven when she died because every day she tried to be a good Motswana woman.

She was thinking about souls, of God and Church, and Father Simon, when Thato pulled her closer to him.

"Sethunya …"

She knew what he wanted, but she was still thinking of Johnnie and she felt like she was going to cry, so she held on tighter to the newspaper to escape Thato's embrace.

"Later. Let me finish reading this," she whispered.

She was thinking that Johnnie must have been so fed up with having people looking at him all day that he snapped. He must have seen the gate open and leapt to freedom, feeling in his heart that he was in a place he did not belong. He yearned for the wide-open veld, with its expanse of earth, where he could snack on leaves plucked from green shrubs. He wanted to close his eyes and enjoy the feel of his mate picking fleas out of his fur; to run freely with others in his troop, the way free chimpanzees do.

Sethunya thought Johnnie just wanted to go home, and even though home was a place that lived only in the depths of his head, he would know when he arrived. He would know when he filled his lungs with clean air that he was truly alive.

"No," she said as she slipped away from Thato's arms. She was tired of trying. She had tried so hard. She had prayed to feel something other than love of a brother for her husband, but she couldn't.

"They killed Johnnie, a chimpanzee at the zoo." She didn't expect Thato to understand the sadness that lived within her and made her impervious to his touch. She knew he couldn't, but she was fine with that because otherwise he was a good husband: patient and kind and generous. He made her feel safe.

When she was young, Sethunya had worn the frilly dresses with tiny flowers her mother dressed her in. And when her mother pinched her thigh and said, "Sit like a girl," she crossed her legs tightly and pulled the skirt over her scabbed knees. But even as she sat in church, listening to the Word, she heard the shouts of the boys who played football down the road. She wished that church would be over so she could go and watch the game.

"Goal-oooo!" they cheered. She wanted so much to play with them but her mother said good girls played netball.

Kgomotso, her best friend, played football. Kgomotso's mother said girls could be anything they wanted to be – just like boys. She walked home with Kgomotso, held her hand, skipped and laughed with her. When the other girls laughed and giggled about boys, she thought only of Kgomotso.

And then one day Kgomotso kissed her, making Sethunya feel warm in places that good girls only whispered about. Goose bumps rose on her arms as her friend ran her hands up and down her back. She felt heat in the tips of her fingers and felt it warm her cheeks.

Sethunya had gone to her friend's home every day after that kiss – wanting more – until a boy from their church saw them and whispered and whispered some more until the words had reached her mother's ears. She wore her saddest face as she spoke to Sethunya.

"Stay away from there, do you hear me? A good girl does not behave that way."

That warning had been enough.

"We can't be friends anymore," Sethunya had told her friend. She enveloped Kgomotso in her heart and tried to send her away, but Kgomotso stayed.

Sethunya prayed. She went to church and knelt in front of the Virgin Mary, praying for forgiveness, but prayer did not tame what she felt. When she did not know where else to turn, she walked into the confessional and, head bowed, she spoke.

"Forgive me Father for I have sinned. It has been too long since my last confession … I've had impure thoughts." She hesitated, and as she did she felt the walls of the tiny room constrict as if to squeeze the sin from her. "I've been with a woman." She heard her heart pounding in her head and added, "And for that I am truly sorry."

Then she waited and the silence grew and filled the room, making her want to flee. But then from behind the curtain, a voice said: "Twenty Hail Mary's my child."

Sethunya had said many more, fervently, and prayer had fortified her weak flesh.

Sethunya read the story about Johnnie again and dabbed the corners of her eyes with the sheet. How silly of her, crying for an animal like it was a person. She thought of Kgomotso then. Sometimes she was a melody that ruffled her memory, or the languidness of a woman's walk.

She was in a kombi once when she thought she saw Kgomotso leaning against a tree. Ebony skin, clean-shaven head and the ever present giant hoops in her ears. One of the passengers said he hated women who pretended to be men. "Look at that one over there," he said, and then he laughed. "That one, all she needs is a real man to teach her how to be a woman." The man in front of her laughed, so did the woman sitting next to her. Sethunya shrank into her seat and took out a lipstick from her bag, smearing mauve over her shame.

Sethunya shook her head to dislodge the thoughts, folded the paper away carefully and placed it on top of the kist. She slid her legs off the bed, slowly, so she didn't wake Thato.

She was tiptoeing out of the room when he spoke: "Tell me, Sethunya."

Sethunya froze, and then she turned slowly to look at him. "Tell you what?"

"Why I make you sad."

She wished Thato hadn't spoken – that he had left her in the far-away place her mind sometimes wandered to, but he was her husband, and so for him she smiled until she felt the smile touch her eyes.

"How can you think that? You don't make me sad. I was just thinking. Sundays do that to me. When I was growing up, Sundays were special. Mama cooked chicken and rice; dessert was guavas and custard. I wore frilly frocks and my mother called Sunday 'The Lord's Day'." She could hear herself bubbling over like a pot of meat on a too-high flame.

"But it is the Lord's Day," Thato said and he sang, softly, for her, the hymn they'd sung at church that morning. Although they had been married five years, his voice still had the ability to halt her mid-sentence. She should have followed him, wrapped her voice around his. She knew that was what he wanted, but at that moment, thoughts of Kgomotso entered her mind, unbidden, unwanted.

"Come." Still she did not move and he said again: "It will be okay, Sethunya."

She sat back down on the bed then. She wished she could shed her unhappiness. She wished, sometimes, he was less good, more like other men who went out drinking nights and returned at dawn, sometimes not at all, who had other women and lied and cheated. If Thato was like that she would have had good reason to leave.

But she knew she would never leave Thato. The thought of life without him immobilised her. That is why she stayed, fighting to keep Kgomotso out of her thoughts, trying not to wish for more. Most times she managed to keep her at bay, but on this night, as she lay with her husband, Kgomotso came alive.

And that is when they chased her. Their feet stomped the earth, spurring her to run, making her flee from outstretched arms that wanted to grab her and tie her down: her mother, Father Simon, sad-eyed women wearing doeks. She ran faster, her mouth gaping, gulping down air to flush out the fear that clogged her lungs. She tripped, but dragged herself up and, as she did, she saw a door at the end of the road. She raced for it and suddenly she felt lighter as the fear lifted her and she was running so fast her feet barely touched the ground. Finally, she was beyond the door. She looked back to find Kgomotso, but as she stood waiting, the door clanged shut; Father Simon locked it and flung away the key.

She woke to Monday morning: the sound of her neighbour's grass broom as the woman swept her yard, kombis hooting, schoolchildren laughing, Thato yawning. He pulled her closer to him and she let him. She felt his warmth, his familiar solidity and steadfastness as he hugged her to him and kissed her forehead.

When he got out of bed, she smiled. She listened to the sound of his slippered footsteps as he padded down the passage to the bathroom. His voice carried over the water spray from the shower as he sang, and she smiled. These were the familiar sounds of her marriage, enfolding her like a blanket on a wintry morning.

She got out of bed and aired the blankets, like her mother had taught her to. She stripped the bed, opened the kist and unfolded the white sheets with pretty pink flowers embroidered on the edge. But as she did, she heard voices begin to sing: *Sethunya likes girls. Sethunya likes girls better.*

A BOY IS A BOY IS A ...

BARBARA ADAIR

South Africa, 1985; civil war, blood, contrition. Perfumed annihilation looms above the station platform that is crammed full, full of lithe brown-clothed soldiers. The boy approaches the ticket counter and buys a one-way ticket to Johannesburg; then he walks up the single line platform. A sign hangs above the platform; it reads JOHANNESBURG: DEPARTING 16H15. It is four o'clock; a train from somewhere has already arrived; it shudders on the platform; smoke rises from beneath it, from silver steel manacled tracks.

The boy steps up into the thin corridor of a train carriage and opens the door of one of the cabins. A family sits in the cabin, a wholesome family made up of parents and 2.6 children, a male husband and a female wife. The husband's face is hairy, unshaved hair that stinks of nicotine and raw marrow, husband eyes, yellow and narrow, bloodstained; his lips are naked and self-doubting. The wife shrinks into the carriage seat; her breasts hang low, drunken; they sway lugubriously in the cabin wind. In her hand she holds a faded pink wet cloth that is covered in lime green vomit. I don't like women, the boy thinks. He watches a hand as it desperately tries to undo the buttons of the woman's tired dress – a child; mean, hungry, worthless. The boy watches the woman as she slaps the child's hand away and pinches its fingers spitefully. What do I feel for little children with mean mothers? the boy wonders as he closes the door and leaves.

He walks on, opens the door of the next cabin. Four women sit on the seats; feral women, cat-eyed; ones who love the sensual life but can never attain it; rainbow eyelids and crude-cut yellow peroxide hair. A woman with long sun-dyed fingernails leans over the wash-basin and plucks her emaciated eyebrows.

"Ouch," she says, "fucking sore this tweezing is." A red scar on her eyelid. She turns to face the door; her breasts leach, ripe watermelons over the top of her naked vest. The woman next to her pushes narrow legs from out of a short purple skirt.

"Not so bad, hey, not so bad," she says. Her legs are smooth, mottled with stains, rounded ankles, corpulent. She winks at him. Is that possible? But the boy knows these passions and disasters; the rages, the debauches, the madness. And so he leaves this cabin too.

Two other women push past him, flatten him against the side of the corridor; a blue dress disrobes her desire, flesh uncovered in the fluorescent light, brushed and taut, feminine, emotional pornography. Too many women, the boy thinks. They smell like flowers, wet flowers; flowers that have had their day in the sun, petals soaked with sweat, used and pressed and hardened.

The boy pushes onwards and opens the next cabin door. Inside are two soldiers, healthy superior, in service to their country; men who kill just like all people kill; soldiers that pillage, wolves that follow the living, knowing that soon there will be a carcass, raw meat; servicemen in sunburnt boots and shoulder ensigns, blue and orange and white, the defence force colours of a nation, a nation of white skins, lepers; they are on a journey to the Holy Land, crusaders. One of them leans forward and holds out his stretched lustrous gun; it shines; dangerous, daring, adoring.

"Come in boy," the other soldier says. He does not hold a gun; instead he leans backwards and stretches out his legs; his cock bulges in the crotch of his pants. "Plenty of space in this cabin. Come sit down, make yourself at home."

Better than the women, the boy thinks. Here I can smell stale sweat and rancid butter; the smell of filth, of life, of heavenly husbands. The boy enters the cabin through the narrow doorway. "Thanks," he mutters.

The boy feels saturated with impudence and entitlement, tragic in a sensuous way. How should I act? he thinks. How does one perform in a setting like this? What kind of variety show do they want? A servile puppy that cringes?

The boy takes a book from his bag, a flat black book with a torn cover, stained, the poetry of Arthur Rimbaud. A schoolteacher gave it to him. He taught him a language, the language of a poet; and the boy, in return, gave the teacher a meaning to these musical sounds. The teacher taught the boy in the time when he did not teach in the classroom; the boy's time of self-obsession and fantastic indulgence, his secret time. And the boy learnt to speak French as if he had been born in France, as if his mother had taught him the tongue while she nursed him at her sweetened breast; he was a Parisian. Now, in this small cabin, the boy holds the book between his reddened fingers and feels indifferent, intimate; he thinks about how he impressed his teacher, such an acute learner. Memory, a boy's memory. How he made the teacher's eyes a nervous blue, his hands sweat and shake; he wanted more; his mouth was sweet and breathy. A boy, nearly a child, his mysterious ways seductive; he spoke a tender talk, remorsefully.

The boy opens the book and turns a page. "But, dear Satan, I beg you not to look at me that way ..."

"What are you reading?" a soldier asks; then he places his gun on his seat and takes the book from the boy's hands. There is no resistance. The soldier's fingers are perfumed with tobacco and brandy; his face is shaven, but not smooth – callous?

"Not even English, weird words," the soldier says. "What are these words, or are you just reading shit and pretending to understand it?"

The soldier turns the pages of the book. "A whole book of it, something funny. Can't even write a proper language, hey? You must be some kind of criminal." The soldier moves his blackened nails over the page; his fingers make a heart-shaped smudge plotted with arteries, blood on a picture of words.

The boy sits forward, and then he shrinks back; difficult to pretend when he is uncertain what the soldier, leering, wants. The boy can't think of the right words to say – a poem, a paragraph of lightning language. I will just pretend breathlessness, the boy thinks; this could mean anything – nervous anticipation, or just a long walk to find a train carriage.

The door opens and a man in civilian clothes enters, sits down. Now there are four of them; the compartment is full, restrictive. The soldier who holds the book passes it to the other, who obsessively caresses his gun.

"Wonder if this young fuck is a queer, a pansy," the soldier winks, or maybe he blinks. "Only a fucking queer reads fucking creepy words like this. And they look like poems. A moffie who can't even speak fucking English properly, this crap."

The soldier with the gun leans forward; the gun presses into him, gently strokes his thigh. He reaches out his hand and takes the book.

"What the fuck are you reading?" the man not in uniform says.

"I'm reading Rimbaud," the boy answers. "He was a poet in Paris, a radical poet. He was shot by a man in the hand once. I was taught by a guy that teaches at the school I went to." The boy knows that he sounds absurd, but he can find no other words; all he can say are the words that he knows, the words that he was taught; a sour bitter truth.

"Paris, France, you mean," one of the soldiers says. "Not Paris, Parys." He laughs; his gums are cherry and his teeth are grey.

The soldier with the gun reaches into the bag beside him and takes out a bottle; the gun moves slightly against his cock as the train starts to move. The boy stares at the metal.

"Hey, don't be afraid boetie," the soldier says. "It's a gun. Not just a gun, but a *gun*." He winks, or maybe he just blinks, again. "Even you have one." He lifts the gun and caresses it; he strokes his cock through the fawn of his pants. "Love my guns. And you?" The soldier laughs again; the other soldier laughs too, and then he pulls at the zip on his pants as if to pull it down and laughs again, loud sounds. The other man looks at them both, and then looks at the boy. Appealing thoughts move in the boy's mind.

The bottle moves to a soldier's lips; his bulging Adam's apple contracts as the brandy follows the curve of his throat, lost, drunk, impure; he passes the bottle. A bead of brown liquid meanders down the other soldier's chin, burning lips; he gulps and coughs. Then the man takes the bottle; a gleam in his eyes, he passes the bottle to the boy.

I'm running away, the boy thinks. I may as well drink poison.

The boy takes the bottle and holds it to his lips; the violence of the venom wracks his limbs, leaves him deformed, baptised. Then the train lurches over something on the track, the bottle flies upwards and the liquid shoots out; falls on a brown boot.

"Hey, fucking creep, queer boy who can't read. Don't fucking waste it, this is good stuff," the soldier whose shirt is streaked with brandy says; then he takes the bottle. A stream of brandy travels down the boot, the delights of damnation.

"Can't waste the stuff," the man says. "Can't waste a drop of fire water." He points at the boy and at the boot. "Come on, lick it up. Can't let it go to waste." The man leans over and pushes on the boy's spine, "Go on lick it up, boy."

The boy feels a frozen passion, crippled. He looks at the soldier who has brandy on his boots; the man not in uniform gestures to him to get down. The other soldier sits; he watches and caresses his gun.

"Come on, lick," the man says; then he pushes the boy downwards. The other soldier leans forward and slowly picks up the gun.

"Come on boy, lick," he says, points the gun at the boy's stomach, "Get down and lick." Dying, the boy thinks, I'm dying. But this kind of death, it feels so good.

The boy lies in mud, criminal; the skin on his scalp is dried to dust, shame, blame; absurd pathetic anger. He senses his seventeen-year-old uncircumcised cock rise; the skin moves. He kneels. Punishment. Power. A soldier pushes at him and the boy lands on his hands and knees, an animal. The boy moves his head downwards, towards the floor, towards the boot; he feels the hard leather lather his tongue; he licks; the brandy smarts on his bare gums; the rawhide foot tastes as if it has been licked before. He opens his mouth wider; he wants to feel the pointed heel against the back of his throat. It seems a long time before he sits up, coughing, debauchery in his emotions. A burden lifts from him; his innocence is forced apart, his wisdom squandered. I am dying, the boy thinks. So all I can do is call my executioners closer. I want to bite the butts of their guns. I am suffocating in sand and blood. Misfortune, this is my god.

"I like this kind of fun," the man in civilian clothes says. "Not so good at doing it myself, but I like to watch." He turns to a soldier. "When did you last fuck a chick? Bet it was a long time ago, hey? You've been in the army and there are no chicks to fuck there. Or did you fuck a terrorist's wife, hey? Hey?" He strokes the soldier's hand, softly, gently.

The soldier laughs. "A cunt is a cunt is a ..." he says, then takes another sip of the brandy. The second soldier takes a cigarette from his pocket.

"I fucked a terr the other day. She stank of fucking animal fat and she cried when I put it in her. She must have been crying from excitement. Ah ...! So I just shoved it up her pussy. It was dry, but the terrs like them dry. They make them dry, adds to the friction. Now I like it dry, very dry. Wonder what the wife will say."

"Let's see the cock," the man says.

The soldier looks at him, "You serious?" he says. The boy gets up from the floor and sits again on the seat; he does not speak. Rimbaud lies on the floor; the pages of a book are stained with brandy and grey ash for a cigarette has fallen on the pristine words.

"I'm serious," the man says. "You said it was big. Let's see. Let's see what you put up a terr's cunt."

"Close the curtains," the soldier says. "Lock the door. Don't want the fucking peanuts and tea girl to bust in on us."

The soldier unzips his pants; he leans over to touch the gun protruding between the other's thighs; his cock bulges; it is circumcised, the skin torn, cut backwards; the pink head faces the ceiling.

"Still not as hard as I can make it," the soldier laughs. He pulls his cock free and holds it; it stays up and then wanders downwards; the red veins gleam in the fluorescent light. "Jesus, can't get it up. Come here queer boy," he calls. "Fix it. Fix it like the French fix it." The soldier takes the boy's hand, holds it to the straining blood. "Touch it, hold it, stroke it." The soldier puts the gun to the boy's forehead, "Come boy, do it."

The boy stares; he feels his blood stir, his head light; he touches the soldier's cock; it feels like a gun; it is a gun; slowly he moves his hand up and down. He bends his head downwards; the tip of his tongue touches glistening glans, a crimson seed; it moves with its own life in the shadowy cabin. The boy lifts up his face; his mouth is open. He feels the metal tip of the silver gun in his mouth; it moves across his neck, onwards, down his back. I am courageous enough to love this pain, the boy thinks. A soldier – who is it? – pulls at the belt that holds up the boy's jeans; the jeans fall to his socks, his red socks. A knife cuts through his underpants. He feels the tip of a gun probe the hole of his arse; he feels the metal move inside him, that deep black hole; it enters. There is no sound except the light that hisses. A soldier pushes him forward and the boy feels the pain. A cock pushes into him; it goes in deeply. Spittle on a hand, semen inside, the smell of unwashed faeces. Another cock; this time it is in his mouth, someone else's. The boy is on all fours; he turns his head upwards; a man's face stares at him; there is a smile on his thin lips, a grimace, a sneer. The boy's mouth fills with the creamy custard flavour of the semen – whose is it this time? It tastes like whipped cream mixed with strawberry jam. He feels his innocence; he loves his innocence.

And then it is finished.

Clickety clack, clickety clack, clickety clack … the wheels of the train underneath him. Now and then the train seems to move over a stone, or maybe just a change in the track. The boy lies in a pool, a puddle of his own blood and sweat and semen, and laughs. He laughs because he knows something more now; he laughs because he feels something more; he laughs because he feels pain and exaltation. It is the power that he laughs about, the ecstasy, sublime power; power that he alone has created, bewitching. He laughs as he thinks of his teacher; he would have been proud, proud and happy to know that he survived, enjoyed the pain; as the teacher enjoyed pain, the pain of rejection by a schoolboy, the pain of a boy's touch. The boy laughs at how much of a simulation it all is, his life a remake. And they were good men these soldiers; they did not kill him.

He gets to his feet. The man looks at him. He puts a finger underneath the boy's chin.

"You did good queer boy. You did good." One of the soldiers licks spittle from his lips and lies back. The other puts his head on the back of the seat; his mouth falls open; his lips are stained brown, nicotine and whisky and semen; a faint whistle emerges from his nose; his eyes are closed; his lips curve into a feeling of satisfaction. The man lies flat on the seat and dreams; he snores. The sound sets fire to grass huts that burn.

The boy picks up his book, the poetry of Arthur Rimbaud; he opens a page; it is torn slightly. Who will love me now, who will love me? the boy thinks. Who will know what I know? Who will know what I can do? I can already feel the pain in my guts. Only I know that this pain is beautiful, that it satiates, that it is divine, that I can do it again. Rimbaud seems docile compared to what he has just done, a girl going to Sunday school, a sweetly sleeping body. The boy closes the book and dreams of the other things that he can do, will do, with guns and soldiers, in calm pale moonlight, a sad beauty; he imagines a marbled fountain, gushing, streaming, sobbing.

The train pulls into Johannesburg station. A soldier pulls his bag from beneath the seat and moves to descend the stairs; the other looks away, his gun held close to his chest. Only the man looks at the boy's eyes. He leans over him.

"You will do it again, I promise," he whispers. "With me next time." And then he too is gone.

The boy rises and leaves the carriage; he climbs down the stairs slowly; he is sore. He stands on the platform and watches the soldiers kiss their mothers, sisters, wives and children.

CHIEF OF THE HOME

BEATRICE LAMWAKA

This story will take me way back. Back to the time before my father's land in Alokolum village became home to thousands of displaced people because of war. To the time we lived in our home, farmed our land, fetched water from the well, cut and gathered wood, and told stories at the evening fire. To the time all Acholi were family, when we ate *malakwang*, vegetables, with our neighbors, *puru awak*, farmed with assistance from the villagers. When we used the word *omera*, brother, and meant it, although you were from another village. All this is changed. Alokolum now hosts iron sheet houses where people peep though the window to see who drives through. Greetings are a thing of the past. Villagers walk as if they are suspicious of one another. We talk about *magendo,* how to make money, not how the family is faring.

This story is about you, Lugul. I am telling your story because I think your story deserves to be heard. Many people may have talked about you but they let your story be buried with the dead. Your story is not the kind of story that is told from generation to generation at the fire. But it is a story that must be told. So I will tell it the way it is. Only I am not at a fire. We no longer tell stories at the fire. And I live in Kampala, three hundred kilometers away from the place I once called home. I only come to Alokolum once a year. I come to the graves of the people I love, and my tears won't stop flowing because

I remember their stories and I may never tell their stories because of the pain it will bring to me. But I will tell your story, Lugul. Your story deserves to be told because you could never tell your own story. Everyone watched what you did. You never told your story. And sometimes I wonder what moral is at the end of it.

Nobody knew which village you came from but everyone called you *omera*. Some people said you were from Paminyai village but nobody confirmed it. Some people said, "Lugul is *lapoya*, a mad man." Others said you were possessed by *cen*, spirits. You didn't tell anyone where you came from or why you moved to Alokolum. I only saw you during the day and never got to know where you spent your nights. You didn't have your own home but everybody welcomed you into their homes. You became part of everyone's home. My mother's hut is where you had most of your meals.

My father said boys should not be close to you because you will teach them how to cook, that you didn't know that being near the cooking fire will burn your penis. Whatever anyone said didn't deter you from doing what you enjoyed most. You continued to fetch water and gather firewood for whoever asked you to. The women loved you. Regina, the woman who had no food in her granary, called you to help her every day. But soon you realised that she wouldn't give you food at the end of the day, so you went to other homes. Some people said Regina had no morals and soon she would make a man of you. Others said you only had a penis, but that wasn't enough to make you a man. I never understood what that meant. I still question what that means.

I always admired how easily you cut wood, but the other girls said, "He is a man so he has a lot of energy to use." I wished that the men in Alokolum would cut the wood and that we would carry it, something that the men shunned because they had been taught that cutting and carrying firewood is a woman's work. My mother never asked Okello, my elder brother, to fetch water. It was also a woman's job so I never expected that of him. You were familiar with the path to the well because you carried water in jerrycans every day, something that my mother wanted my father to do but it was only wishful thinking. Like her mother, she had been told to provide whatever her husband needed. I watched her toil each day as my father drunk lacoyi, home brew, with other men in the evening. At the end of the day he complained he was exhausted and my mother never said a word.

My mother called you to our home every day when we were about to eat. She knew you needed a place to call home. She called you her assistant because you helped when she needed something done. I would look for you until I found you, then we would eat. You always said *apwoyo*, thank you, after every meal. My father never said thank you to my mother and it was funny to hear you appreciate my mother's cooking. My father always complained about the salt or the *odii*, groundnut paste, but you never did.

I remember the day you came to our home because you heard my mother screaming. She was being beaten by my father because she said there was no money to buy his *lacoyi*. I was glad you came to help my parents stop the fight, although that wasn't the last time they fought. You became the *latek*, a peace builder, of the village. Whenever there was a fight between a husband and wife you came to help the woman. I don't know why you decided to do that, but I am sure a lot of women were grateful to you. You had begun what a lot people didn't bother to care about, because to them a fight between two lovers wasn't anyone's business.

I was about ten years old when you appeared in Alokolum. I saw you carry firewood on your head. I asked my mother why my father doesn't do that. Her only reply was, "*En rwot gang*, he is chief of the home." And when I asked her why you were not *rwot gang*, she scolded me for asking too many questions. That day, I decided you were my friend and I wanted to know why you were not *rwot gang*.

I sneaked from home when my mother was cooking the evening meal. I looked for you. It was not hard to find you. You were at Korina's house splitting firewood with an axe. I watched as you lifted the axe easily and the wood separated. Korina paid you with *arege*, homemade gin. You sat close to her hut while other men sat under the mango tree to drink *arege*. You didn't join like other men did when they arrived later. You were more interested in what the women were talking about. Even though the men called you, "*Lugul bin imat arege ii kin coo*, Lugul come and drink alcohol with your fellow men," you ignored their call.

You didn't say anything when one man, drunk with *arege*, said, "*Lugul obedo dako ma lacoo*, Lugul is a woman man." You seemed not to mind whatever people called you. You never answered the men when they insulted you. You murmured and walked away. Some men called you a coward. I didn't think you were coward. I just wanted you to say something mean to them. You didn't seem to notice me as I followed you down the village path. You never once stopped and asked why I followed you around. You only turned and looked me, and then I saw a smile appear on your lips. I knew that was our connection. You were my friend and I would be yours.

When the new government took power you went to Gulu town. Many people in the village moved away. My father said Alokolum was our home and we would stay there. We watched as people carried their luggage on their heads to safety. We heard the gunshots and the bombs but we stayed in Alokolum. At night we left home and slept in the bush. I never complained because I felt safe, although I worried about finding snakes in my bedding. I was happy when we moved back home because nothing had happened in the village. Nobody talked about why you left. You may have left the same way you came. We didn't see you around Alokolum anymore. One of the villagers saw you at Gulu. You were helping, cleaning around. You swept the streets, picked up rubbish as you did in Alokolum. The soldiers shot you with six bullets because they suspected that you were a spy.

Today, I stand at your graveside here on my father's land. Your grave is well maintained. Somebody has pulled up the unwanted plants. I remember when nobody wanted your corpse buried at their home. You did work and helped people do what most people hated to do. A lot of people thought you were mad. Some said you were not comfortable with your sexual manhood. That doesn't matter now. When the news of your death came to Alokolum, my father said he would give you a home where you will rest. He said you were a good man but the world didn't treat you well. I never understood his change of heart. Maybe he knew deep down in his heart, although the harsh words never stopped coming from him.

He now lies next to you. He died during the war because he wanted to treat people who were injured, sick. He wanted to stand by the people of Alokolum. He didn't stop when he received warnings from the soldiers that he was supporting the rebels even though the rebels came into his home and stole his medication. The soldiers shot him in the head and left him to die. My father may have been motivated by you to help people. He died helping people.

But this story is not about my father. It is your story. It is a story about the man that the villagers didn't get to know. I wish that a lot of men could do what you did. Nobody knew where you came from. You have found a home in a new world. Nobody wanted to call you a man because you fetched water from the well, carried firewood on your head. Today, I will call you my hero because you did what you wanted to do. You were *rwot gang*.

PINCH

MARTIN HATCHUEL

Pinch was the game they invented when they were boys running together on the veld behind their village in the wild and lonely Karoo, the only boys in their tiny settlement where Meiring's father ran the district's post office and trading store and Ludolf's father drank the *mampoer* he distilled under an overhang in the valley half a day's easy ride from his house. Pinch was when you sneaked up on your opponent without him seeing or hearing you and you caught the delicate skin at the side of his neck or under his arm between your thumb and forefinger and you twisted; and, of course, Pinch turned back on you if you were caught before you pinched.

And that was what made Pinch so addictive: they knew each other so well that it was almost impossible to succeed. They could feel each other, the one when the other came close; they knew each other's needs, each before the other knew his own; they saw the world together, each through the eyes of the other.

As he lay in the cold and the dark, Ludolf tried to remember their scores. Meiring had always been in the lead, always a little more secure, a little more cunning, but he'd had his turn and there were times, satisfying, shout-inducing, laugh-till-you-hurt times when Ludolf had Pinched first and won (and when he'd lost he'd had to take his punishment: Meiring with his neck in an arm lock, drilling his knuckles into the poll of his head and shouting, "Give up yet?

Give up?" And Ludolf would never give up and he'd wrestle back, hooking his leg and tripping them both until they landed giggling in the dust and panting in each other's arms).

They hadn't played Pinch since they'd joined the commando almost eighteen months ago.

Meiring stirred in his sleep. Ludolf could smell his animal smell and felt the rough, filthy cloth of his jacket against his cheek. He tried to tuck their blanket under his shoulder behind him and he reached over and tried to push the far corner over Meiring's chest. But it was too small. He felt the cold come in from behind, down his legs and into his boots and creeping up his back from the crack where his trousers had parted from his shirt. There was nothing he could do but push their bodies closer together to try and draw what he could from Meiring's warmth.

The smell was nothing: they'd got used to the stink of each other long ago and they'd got used to sleeping in pairs like this, sleeping as all the men did when they were on commando and the nights in the veld were cold beyond cold and a fire was unthinkable and they had nothing but each other for warmth. But Ludolf had never got used to Meiring's body. It was too close. It was too fine.

Meiring moaned and sighed and opened his eyes. "Mmh," he said, his mouth thick with sleep. "Still dark."

"It's almost morning." The moon was a thin line in the sky, and they'd slept in the starlight but now the colour was growing in the east.

"I'm cold," said Meiring and pushed himself backwards against Ludolf. But Ludolf had to hold himself away, hold the lower part of himself away so that Meiring wouldn't feel his hardness. He felt bad as soon as he'd moved like that and made up for it by putting his arm around Meiring's shoulder and hugging his chest against his broad, strong back.

Meiring looked back at him and smiled. "We'd better get up," he said, and reached back to pat him on his thigh and rolled himself onto his knees and stood. Then he walked a few steps and stopped and peed on the ground. It sounded steamy and loud in the clear, still air.

This was their second night away from their commando and they were hungry. They'd been living on biltong and *beskuit* for months and they'd been riding quickly in the last few days, stopping less than normal because they expected they were being followed by enemy patrols and here, close to Graaff-Reinet and deep in the Colony, they were running low on ammunition and the commandant wanted to avoid any fighting until after they'd met up with the rest of their column, hoped they'd find them waiting somewhere near Bethesda with supplies and, perhaps, news from home. There were sympathisers in Bethesda, he'd said, a family of Rebels he thought he knew.

And then when it was getting close to dawn and the night was dark and the clouds hid the moonlight and the stars, Meiring and Ludolf had got lost. They'd been riding through a *poort* filled with unseasonable mist, close at each other's side as always, leading one another until in a sudden clearing they'd realised they were alone and that they'd probably been alone for some hours.

They'd stopped at a pool and allowed their horses to drink as the dawn grew around them and Meiring had said, "I think we should wait here for the light. Rest a while. Then we can go back and try and work out where the others have gone."

But the resting had been good and they were exhausted and this was the first time the two of them had been alone in months and they'd felt safe like that, hidden amongst the rocks and the bushes. "We'll move on tomorrow," Meiring had said.

And now tomorrow was here.

"Have we got anything left to eat?" he said, turning as he buttoned his flies.

"I've got one piece of biltong and two or three pieces of beskuit," said Ludolf.

"Same here," said Meiring.

Ludolf was kneeling, rolling their blanket in their canvas groundsheet and tying the bundle with a worn strip of leather. A horse and saddle each; a rifle each; a hat each and a set of clothes; and a single blanket and a groundsheet – between them that was everything they had.

"Maybe we should wait until tonight and try and find a farm and see if they've got anything there," he said. "Maybe they can give us directions."

"Good idea," said Meiring, "if they're on our side. And anyway we can't ride during the day this close to Graaff-Reinet: the Khakis might see the dust." It hadn't rained and the clouds had gone and the soil of the veld was powdered and red. They were surrounded by red and by the dull military green of the Karoo's stunted, rounded shrubs and the pale, fragile white of its waves of tall and delicate grass.

They ate what they had, sharing as they always did, knowing they'd be hungry again in an hour or two, and then they took water straight from the pool and drank.

"You know what?" said Meiring. "Let's stay here another day. We can wash our clothes. We both need to wash our clothes."

"We'll never catch the others then. We're too far behind."

"I know," said Miering, and he grinned.

They were friends and they were equals, but Meiring had always taken the lead like this. And it wasn't just his age: he'd always been quicker than Ludolf, less trusting of others but also more daring, before the war always first with ideas for adventures, always leading them into trouble – and often leading them out again. But in the eighteen months since they'd become men by joining the fight (and they were hardly that: Meiring, older by a year, had turned seventeen on the day they'd ridden out), Meiring had aged the quicker of the two. The days and weeks of waiting, then suddenly riding too quickly to another place to wait again, the tension before the bullets began to scream into the men around them, the hot terror of the shrapnel and the noise of the cannons that frightened them and thundered into their souls; the farms burning and the livestock dead, shot by the enemy and left to rot; the parties of women and young children and old men that tramped the veld – these things had changed them all but they'd changed Meiring more than most and he'd become distant and silent.

And now here was the old Meiring again and Ludolf was pleased and relieved. And he'd decided he'd Pinch him at least once before the day was out.

Suddenly Meiring punched his shoulder.

"Hey!" and Ludolf punched him back.

"Ha!" said Meiring. "Eighteen months on commando and you still hit like a girl!"

Ludolf threw himself at him, struggling for a grip at his arms and pinning him down. They were both short for their age but they were lean, lean from being teenagers and lean from their hunger, and they had teenage spirit and they wrestled fiercely. They began to shout as they fought, smiling first at each other and then laughing louder and louder until suddenly Ludolf felt Meiring go limp beneath him.

"Giving up, are you?"

"No," said Meiring. "We need to be quiet."

"Oh," said Ludolf, letting go of the older boy's wrists and sitting back astride him, feeling the softness and the flatness and the surprising slimness of his waist under his thighs and looking down at him and resting there a moment before rolling off and lying next to him to stare up at the sky. It was blue now and the sun was filling it from where it was coming up above the ridge to the east.

"If we wash early, our clothes'll dry quicker," he said.

"We'll need to keep watch," said Meiring. "Let's wait until it's a bit warmer, then you can go in first."

"Let's climb up there in the meantime," said Ludolf and he pointed at the ridge. "See where we are."

They checked on their horses, loose-hobbled and grazing, and they took their rifles and their bandoliers and put on their hats and began to walk.

It was easy going across the valley, a bit tricky on the scree at the bottom of the slope. Ludolf let Meiring lead the way, as always, and soon they found a game path and they started to climb. It was a low ridge and they came suddenly to the top and Meiring ducked down so that his head wouldn't show against the sky.

"What's there?" whispered Ludolf.

Meiring waved his hand for silence. He raised his head again and slowly panned the veld as he stood there, hunched and stiff and Ludolf could see the concentration in the tension of his body.

"Nothing," he said after a long time and as he did, Ludolf grabbed the skin on his neck and Pinched and twisted. And then he giggled that high-pitched, rising laugh he gave when he was excited and he turned and started to run.

"You bliksem!"

They tore down the path, careening and out of control, their legs and arms pumping uncoordinated, rifles waving, shouting and whooping, their voices echoing in the silence of the morning. Ludolf had the lead as they ran across the riverbed and Meiring dropped his weapon and launched at him and tackled him and brought him down.

"Pinch," said Meiring when they'd caught their breath and the laughter had died. "I'd forgotten about Pinch."

"Do you still remember the score?" said Ludolf.

"Of course I do. Forty to me, one to you."

"Rubbish!" said Ludolf. "You're crazy."

"Pinch," said Meiring, and there was a sadness in his voice. "Pinch," he said again. "I'd forgotten about Pinch."

It was hot in their valley with the sun overhead and they were sweating and ready to swim. "But we have to stop making so much noise," said Meiring.

"You said you didn't see anything," said Ludolf.

"I dunno. I saw the town."

"What? Graaff-Reinet?"

Meiring nodded. "It's about six miles from here."

"Dear Jesus." He knew they were in the enemy's country, but Graaff-Reinet – that was the biggest garrison of all.

"It'll be okay," said Meiring. "You go first, but just be quiet. Don't splash or anything. I'll keep watch from that rock over there and I'll throw a stone if I see anything," and he stood up and picked up his rifle and his feet crunched softly on the sharp, clean sand.

Ludolf fiddled with his rifle and turned his back to Meiring and undressed and then collected his clothes into a ball in front of himself and turned and let himself slowly into the muddiness of the water.

It was warm in the shallows but colder as it got deeper, and he lay back and let it cover him, all of him except his nose and his eyes. It was good. Then he took his pants and rubbed them against themselves under the water and did the same with his shirt and his jacket and swished them around and lifted them up and grinned at Meiring and Meiring grinned back at him and waved.

He found a stone and rubbed his skin with it and then when he was finished and he couldn't hide any more, he came out of the water still with his back to Meiring and spread his clothes on a bush in the sun to dry.

"Come here, it's my turn," said Meiring and Ludolf had no choice, he had to walk naked across the sand to where Meiring was sitting on the rock and he picked up his rifle for something to hold as he went.

Meiring watched and laughed as he sat down and jumped up again when the hot stone burned his naked skin. "You'll have to sit on your hat, guy."

Ludolf made himself comfortable and Meiring began to undress. They'd seen each other naked often before; at home they'd taught themselves to swim by pushing each other into the deepest pools in the river and since they'd joined up they'd swum together with the other men in the commando and if Meiring thought there was anything strange about Ludolf's sudden shyness today, he said nothing about it.

Ludolf tried not to watch but he was transfixed by the broad slabs of muscle on Meiring's hairless chest, by the small, tight nipples, crowns on their own dark circles, by the lithe, white stomach, the thin march of hair down to the navel, the dark triangle in which his manhood nested like a short, thick, blunt-ended rope.

His mouth went dry and his stomach clamped down and he realised he was getting hard and he was guilty and he thought What is this? and whatever it was he was sure it was sin. They talked a lot and listened to the men when they lay around in their laagers or when they rode out together, and the older men sometimes spoke about the evils and hungers of the flesh, and the dominees had thundered about them whenever they'd listened to a sermon (less regularly at home, where they saw their dominee only when he travelled through or when their fathers took them to town for shopping and *Nachtmaal* – but on commando they had them amongst them and they heard them all the time). But none of them had ever said anything about anything like this.

Why was he feeling this? Why suddenly? Why today? Why?

And yet he felt love.

Meiring took much longer to rinse his clothes and to swim than Ludolf had done and he lay on his back and took water into his mouth and spurted it towards him like a statue in a fountain, said nothing as he lay for minutes looking at Ludolf on the rock, turned over and stroked once or twice across the pool, the pale globes of his backside glistening where they caught the sun through the mud in the water.

When he was done he stood on the bank and flicked water from his skin and then he spread his clothing on the shrubs next to Ludolf's. He felt the other boy's jacket and said, "Your stuff's almost dry," and then he came across to the rock and leaned against it and turned his face towards the sun, closing his eyes against the glare.

Later they dressed and lay in the shade and slept and waited for the heat to pass.

Towards evening they checked on the horses again and took them to the water to drink. Then Ludolf saw a rabbit in the riverbed and he risked the noise and shot it. Meiring skinned it and gutted it and said, "We'll have to wait till it's dark before we light a fire; we don't want them to see the smoke." They collected wood and kindling in the last of the day and then when it was dark they lit the fire with a flint but it was too small and they cooked too quickly and they were too hungry and the sweet gamy meat tasted raw and bloody when they ate it.

Ludolf didn't want the night to come, scared of lying down with Meiring after the things of today but Meiring was tired when they'd eaten and said, "It's too late to go anywhere now; we might as well sleep here and ride out in the morning."

Ludolf was casual. "We'll have to leave early then," he said.

"Before the dew," said Meiring. "Before the dew."

The cold came quickly under that crystal, cloudless sky, the brittle starlight brighter and the insects rattling louder than ever before as Ludolf and Meiring pulled their blanket closer around them.

"Do you ever think of home?" said Meiring.

"Of course I do," said Ludolf. "Don't you?"

"All the time."

"You remember when we got into your father's still that time and drank his mampoer?"

"How can I forget it? I've never had such a headache in all my life."

"Did you know he knew we'd done it?"

"No, he didn't."

"Yes, he did."

"But how did he find out?"

"I told him."

"Why did you go and do that?"

"I thought you were going to die. I told him so he'd know why you were sick."

"He never said anything to me."

"I made him promise he wouldn't."

"But he would have thrashed me if he'd known."

"He thrashed me instead."

Ludolf was lying behind Meiring and he sat up and leaned over his shoulder and looked down at him.

"Never."

"He did. Think I'd lie about it?"

"No, I don't suppose you would."

But Meiring's voice was getting weaker and soon his breathing slowed and deepened and Ludolf knew he'd fallen asleep.

They'd spent so many nights like this and they were used to the hard ground beneath them and they usually slept easily, but tonight Ludolf was restless and he had to force himself to lie still or Meiring would wake. He didn't want to wake him: he wanted to protect him and make him comfortable and keep him safe. And as soon as the thought came to him, he felt himself growing and he was disturbed by his powerful hardness and the tenderness at its tip as it rubbed and pushed against his trousers and against the small of Meiring's back.

The rest day had tired him, though, and at last he slept.

His bladder woke him sometime in the night when everything was silent and he pulled himself slowly away from their bed and walked a way off and tried to pee without sound. He shivered as he stood and waited for the flow and he was cold when he came to lie down again and as he lay up against Meiring the boy moved back towards him and snuggled against him as he had this morning and they slept again.

Later Ludolf woke a second time and they'd changed positions in their sleep. Now he was lying on his right side and Meiring was behind him, his body pressed tight against his own, knees behind knees, his hand on Ludolf's shoulder. And Ludolf's eyes grew wide as he realised Meiring's hardness was pressing against him, too, and that it was warm through the layers of their clothing.

Ludolf lifted his head and craned his neck to look back and Meiring was smiling. He lay down again and looked straight ahead and he was shivering, but not because he was cold.

Suddenly Meiring's hand moved onto his chest and he felt himself pulled even closer and he pushed himself back against him, pushed with his backside against his hardness and it was good.

He feels it too, he thought. He feels it too. And his heart beat in his ears and his eyes filled and he squeezed them tight and he thought about kissing him. He'd never kissed anyone before, but he knew what it was and he didn't care, in the morning when they woke he'd kiss him.

But it was a footfall that woke them and men talking in the strange, sing-song language of the enemy. English. Neither of the boys spoke English.

"Here they are, sir!"

Five Khakis surrounding them, a sixth leading their horses. One of them holding their rifles.

"Where are the rest of your troop, boys?"

"What's he saying?" whispered Meiring.

"I don't know," said Ludolf.

"It seems they don't speak English, sir."

"I can see that, sergeant, thank you."

"Sir."

"Well, get them up!"

The sergeant came closer and took a corner of the blanket between his thumb and forefinger, cautiously as if it was diseased, his nose pulled up, took it and pulled it away and let it fall and motioned them to stand.

"This one's wearing British insignia," he said, pointing at Meiring. "Sir! Look at the jacket. He stole it from the 17th!"

"I can see that, too, sergeant," said the officer. He reached across himself and opened the holster at his side and rested his hand on the butt of his pistol.

"You read Lieutenant-Colonel Gorringe's orders, sergeant. If the enemy wears our insignia, it's a capital offence. Execute him."

"But a trial, sir, what about a trial?"

"Why's he getting his gun out?" said Ludolf.

But Meiring said nothing.

"Oh, they'll get their trial, sergeant. They always get their trial."

Meiring turned to look deeply at Ludolf as the officer drew his weapon and pointed it directly at his beautiful, blonde head. And then he smiled at the boy he loved and said, once and sadly,

"Pinch."

IN THE WAY SHE GLIDES

MERCY MINAH

She was not meant to walk on land, Ms J thought. Standing head and shoulders above everybody in the crowds milling about the corridor lockers, the girl lumbered awkwardly down the corridor, with her broad shoulders and back. Ms J followed at an inconspicuous distance. She was almost certain she walked alone. But talking to her now would create the wrong impression; the other students would assume she was in some kind of trouble again. She didn't like the school much, with its uppity kids always reporting the girl for stealing their lunch and bullying them for money. It was obvious that she was poor, yet they all made such a fuss. Ms J wove through the crowds without being bothered by any of the students. She too wasn't very popular with them.

None of the other sports coaches was interested in taking the girl on. "She's too clumsy for basketball," said one. "She's too big for netball," said another. And girls weren't allowed to play soccer. But Ms J knew, the moment she laid eyes on Pippa Jacobs, that she had found the star swimmer for the school's team. She saw it in the large, powerful arms and shoulders. She saw it in the broad back and thick firm neck. She saw it in the small, close-shaved head. Ms J saw it in the girl's impressive chest, which stood a good distance away from her godlike body. She saw it in the taut bum, forever buried in loose-fitting tracksuit pants or gym shorts. With every other swimmer she put on the team, she had had to witness actual aquatic skills. But with Pip it was different.

Pip walked past the locker corridor, having been ignored by everyone, and kept her head low until she stepped into the sunshine outside. Ms J followed her past the deserted classrooms, past the big sports field, and waited until Pip wandered into the teachers' parking lot. She enjoyed watching the girl's receding form, that impressive broad back. It created an urgency in her that she hadn't felt in ages; she had always had a weakness for large women.

"Jacobs!" she called out, as Pip walked towards the parked cars. Seemingly unfazed by Ms J's sharp tone, Pip turned slowly and gave her a crooked smile. She had badly shaped teeth that were clustered together, some overlapping the others.

"Yes Miss?" the girl said, in a voice that made it sound like she was laughing at a secret joke – at your expense.

Pip had silver-grey eyes, which seemed to blur the harshness of everyday life and numb out some untold pain. Ms J knew that her home life was riddled with the dysfunction that was typical of poor families. What if Pip laughed at her? Would she be able to handle the rejection? What rejection? Pip was just a child; she was only asking her to swim.

"I'd like you to meet me at the pool on Monday. Two-thirty. Sharp. Bring a swimming costume," Ms J said, trying not to make it obvious that her knees had gone weak at the thought of Pip in a swimming costume, one that would cling to her large frame, pretending to cover her, but revealing all. It took Ms J a moment to realise that Pip was walking away. The urgency rose up in her again, this time in her chest. "Well? Will you come?" she asked, hating and liking the whine in her voice.

Pip looked puzzled. For a moment Ms J feared that the entire exchange may have taken place in her head. But before she could rectify this, Pip's mouth curved into that crooked smile of hers again.

"Oh, I thought I had said, No problem miss. Guess I only said it in my head."

Ms J searched the silver-grey eyes and dull face for a sign of insolence, found none, and smiled back. A rare and easy smile. "I can't wait to start work on you, Pip."

That crooked smile again. Then, as if she didn't want to have to stick around for a moment longer, she was sprinting away in a thunderous run.

Ms J turned in a sulk – too quickly to see Pip look back at her with a crooked smile and an arched eyebrow. By then she was half regretting her decision to speak to Pip at all. Chances were the girl couldn't even swim. She should have been looking for a new swimmer among the girls already suggested to her. Girls who had come prepared, with their kits and their years of swimming experience. Girls she had told to go home as she had already found the new swimmer.

Ms J lived alone in Salt River, an industrial suburb near Table Bay. Her house was a small two-bedroom affair, one road down from the school, with a pool. She did a couple of lengths of breast-backstrokes in it to ease her nerves. She drank a glass of wine. Just one. Then she tried to call her children. The phone rang for a long time. Someone picked up just as she was replacing the receiver. It sounded like Jenna. Or was it Lauren?

It was six years since Ms J's ex-wife Martha had left with her daughters, months since she had last seen them. They had visited her in Phoenix House – the alcohol rehab centre –- for a while, but then the visits had stopped. She had not called them to let them know that she had completed her programme, moved back to Cape Town and found a job.

She thought of how her marriage had fallen apart, how she had begun to fall out of love with Martha and the girls, and in love with the warmth and security – it sounded so sick and pathetic now – of booze. Martha had found someone else to fill up the empty spaces she had created through her affair with alcohol, and soon there was just no love. When Martha, the girls and this someone else had come home for the umpteenth time to find Ms J sprawled across the kitchen floor in her own vomit, cradling a bottle of gin, everyone understood that the marriage was over. The divorce was swift and simple, the lawyers a little too pleased that the rainbow-nation marriage had come to an end and Richard had already moved in. All he had to do – once the divorce was finalised – was legally adopt the girls. Which he did within three months. Ms J was cast out into the streets with conditional visitation rights and no claim for maintenance. The conditions were a fulltime stay in rehab and a visible recovery. She had worked hard to achieve both of these, as well as to rebuild her sense of self worth.

The coaching job had come easily. She was a white, middle-aged, single woman. She had a thin, toned body and a voice that cut through the air like a whip. She had no experience as a coach, but she did have a bunch of medals to show that – at some point in her life – she knew more than a thing or two about swimming. That was seven months ago, and Ms J had built a strong enough team to compete with other schools. But none of the girls was good enough to win. And then she had her epiphany about Pip. The girl's silver-grey eyes and the awkwardness with which she moved on land convinced her that Pip was meant to glide in water. Large and notorious, Pip. Poor and androgynous, Pip. Not very smart and almost antisocial, Pip.

Monday rolled around cold, windy and slow. Only three girls showed up for the meet: Roxanne, Michelle and Pip. She looked ridiculous in her swimming costume: bright pink with long frills around the shoulders and legs, obviously borrowed. It looked as though it had sleeves and a little tutu. It clashed with the startling silver of Pip's eyes. Ms J could have wept; this was not the Pip she had had in mind.

The two smaller girls wore plain black numbers and stood with grim expressions on their faces, staring straight ahead. Pip slouched a bit, crooked grin lingering. Her arms and legs looked much softer than Ms J had imagined, with very little muscle tone, and almost no definition. She looked large and stupid; a seventeen-year-old dyke in a five-year-old's swimming costume. Ms J had made a terrible mistake. But she had to go ahead.

"Take your places," Ms J said. Then she studied, as she always did, the face of each girl. Roxanne stared at the water with an arrogance many believed would make her a star. Michelle, one of Ms J's best swimmers, smiled a little at it, daring it to make things difficult for her. Her eyes moved to Pip. A change had taken place in the girl's face. Her eyes shone, her chapped lips were set in a thin line over her teeth, a bead of perspiration slid down her nose. She stood very still, upright, stretching her neck and holding her chin up. Her short, stubby fingers played with the air, as though fluttering over the keys on a piano.

"Alright, women! I want you swim three laps in a row. I'll meet you on the other side of the pool. Freestyle!" Ms J barked in her coach voice.

None of the girls showed any sign of disapproval or indignation. It was a cold day and Ms J had just asked them to swim three laps in cold water. Ms J liked tough.

Roxanne's dive was flawless. Her body arched inwards and her pointed fingertips hit the water first, paving the way for the rest of her slight frame. She chose the breaststroke. Michelle's dive was just as perfect, and she chose the butterfly. Both girls made medium splashes, creating small dark patches of wetness on the concrete around the pool. Ms J bit her lip as she readied herself for Pip's dive. The large girl raised herself onto her toes and bent her knees before arching into the water. It was a clean, flowing movement. The tiny droplets she left disappeared fast. The dives took place seconds apart, yet Ms J was able to capture each movement as though watching them in slow motion. Even though the other two girls had a head start, Pip closed in on them fast, the water sliding down and over her back easily. She didn't seem to fight against it like the others. It seemed to welcome her and propel her forward. She was the first to touch the pool wall. The other two decided to change styles, but Pip stuck to her fast crawl.

Ms J stared. Her chest constricted and her heart rate accelerated. It was like magic the way the girl and the water worked in unison. Her body was taut and her movements were crisp, making the pink costume more eccentric than ever. Soon Ms J was giving Pip her undivided attention, watching with dilated pupils and intense concentration how the girl's muscles rippled through the clear, sparkling water. She could feel her lower stomach contract in the beginnings of sexual arousal as Pip's body glided through the water. Pip swam alone in her third lap – speed and strength – the others trailing far behind.

Ms J ran, laughing, to the other side of the pool and stuck her hand into the water, ready to take Pip's. The girl had the look of exhilaration, and she heaved her out of the water and grabbed her in an uncharacteristic bear hug. Pip was panting and grinning from ear to ear. Ms J grinned back at her.

"That was marvellous," Ms J exclaimed. "Where'd you learn to swim like that?" She was very excited – in more ways than one.

"When we were kids, my sister and I would go down to the river and swim. We live on the west side of the railway station. I've been swimming since I was little," Pip said, her heavy Afrikaans accent obvious to Ms J for the first time.

She watched Pip walk away to towel herself on the benches next to the pool. Ms J shook her head in disbelief. Pip was a born swimmer.

Both Ms J and Pip were oblivious to Roxanne's angry frown. This girl was not going to mess up Roxanne's chances in the world of swimming. She would have to keep a close eye on Ms J and her new little friend, Pippa Jacobs.

ROCK

LINDIWE NKUTHA

Now as far as music goes, I've always preferred rock and roll and nothing else. I love the kind of guitar sound that makes my head pull my heart muscles in different directions. In fact, I've always dreamt of one day learning to play the guitar, just like my mother. Even though she has not played in a long time. I guess this is how the nickname Rock stuck to me. I should really say I hope that is how. The truth is different, though, and it wears many faces. One version of it, which I suspect is truer than most, has a little something to do with the fact that I have been rocking and rolling all my life. On my makeshift wheelchair, that is, since I was seven. Throughout my childhood I have had to make peace with the children in my neighbourhood whispering "Rock 'n Roll" every time I rocked and wheeled myself from my house to the shops, and from school back to my house again.

I lost both my legs to hunger. Thanks to the ravenous appetite of our neighbour's dog, which had not been fed for over a week, my legs were mistaken for lamb shank. As a teenager I came to convince myself that it was no intentional ill-feeling on the dog's part, just hunger that could not be ignored. I could relate to that. There had been moments in my life when I, too, had been so hungry I had fantasised about eating the same dog. I guess the dog got to what was on both our minds before I did, and I thought that was fair. This thought reminded me of the writing on a bumper sticker pasted on the back of a guitar that stood next to my mother's bed, the same one she had not played in years. EAT OR BE EATEN, it said.

My mother, ever the erratic pragmatist, did not share this philosophical analysis of my fate, and was determined to sue our neighbours for my deformation, in a way similar to what she had seen people do on American television. Had it not been for Malum' Justice's intervention, she might actually have gone ahead and done just that.

It was Malum' Justice, my mother's younger brother, and the only member of my family to have spent more than two semesters at a university in his short-lived attempt to study the law, who pointed out to his sister that in order to sue one had to have some money in the first place.

"To pay the lawyers, Sis' Ncedi," he said in a voice befitting a freshly-struck-off-the-roll barrister, in answer to the Why? question that never quite made it out of my mother's lips.

It was a fact that did not need stating that Sis' Ncedi did not have any determinable coins to rub together. In fact, there were church mice that had managed a level of affluence greater than hers, by both human and mouse standards.

There are a lot of things that I find do not make a lot of cents. I mean, sense, in my head. The list, if I cared enough to produce one, would stretch to the horizon. So every now and then I allow different puzzlers to drift in and out of my mind. Just last week I was wondering about two things in particular. The first was why it is that people with money find it necessary to rub coins against each other. The second was why my mother, who – as I have already said – was a woman who did not have any coins to call her own, let alone rub together, had wanted to sue people who at the time had even less than she.

Bra Phandi's dog was the neighbourly culprit.

Bra Phandi was the sort of fellow who fit neatly into the government's newspeak-inspired definition of previously and currently disadvantaged. A feat which life had accomplished for him when the Unharmonious gold mine closed down and lost him his job. Exactly six years before his dog mistook me for Sunday lunch.

Sis' Ntokozo, Bra Phandi's wife and sole breadwinner for that same period, had over the years developed a case of arthritis so severe that the only comfortable position she could find for her hands was suspending them in the air. This habit gave her an aura of a piano maestro straining to decide which concerto to play next. So acute was her condition that the flood of laundry which once had flowed into her house demanding that she wade through it for pay, if pay is what it could be called, soon dried up and made them first runners-up in the privation contest.

All of that changed, though, when Bra Phandi, realising that their condition was not about to alter itself any time soon, decided to make peace with the hand that life had dealt him. To his credit he took over his wife's duties and established himself as the neighbourhood's first male washerwoman – a move which at once earned him instant brownie points with all the womenfolk and again opened up the floodgates of laundry.

Suggestive grunts referring to him as Auntie Phandi soon vanished into the communal gut of swallowed words, when he decided to be entrepreneurial about his new vocation. The first thing to show that he meant business was the improvised billboard; then the ubiquitous pamphlets bearing his name and the services he offered. These were handed out house-to-house at every street corner by his overzealous army of sales representatives (neighbourhood children aching to supplement their non-existent weekly allowances). He paid fifty cents for every distributed pamphlet that resulted in actual business. In no time, our whole area was awash with BRA PHANDI WASHERWOMAN ENTERPRISES. In one stroke Bra Phandi had managed to turn the mundane business of washing other people's clothes into a lucrative business and a piece of news over which countless cups of tea were drunk.

"At least he is being responsible and manly enough to take care of his wife. Something we can't say about the lot of you," Green Mamba used to say.

Green Mamba was a woman who lived two streets away from us, and who was a friend of no one in particular. As I heard it, she ordinarily went by the name Jacqoubeth when she was not called otherwise by my uncle.

Malum' Justice used to say, "There is nothing else that anyone who walks around wearing a skunky towel so green and worn-out that it brings up images of a snake shedding deserves to be called other than Green Mamba."

He presented a very persuasive case. So, in my mind too, Jacqoubeth began to exist as Green Mamba.

"At least she is nothing like your work-shy, beer-thirsty, stingy-backside-linked-to-a-head-full-of-a-tiny-knowledge-of-the-law, Justice!" my mother said as a rejoinder in support of the Green one, every time Malum' Justice expressed a different opinion. He had made it his business always to do just that. He called it the art of being contrary. In his larynx he carried a barrage of retorts, which he had perfected the art of administering. Not a word was lost with him. He was so particular about his words that he would not utter a single one unless he knew that its departure from his lips was destined for the bulls-eye. Where it hurt the most. When he felt defeated by my mother – and this was seldom – he always resorted to asking her the one question he knew she wasn't too open to entertaining.

"Awusho Ncedi, do you ever intend restringing that guitar which has been showing us its armadillo smile for what is beginning now to feel like eternity?"

He knew that if there was a line guaranteed to silence my mother and make surly her mood, that was the one.

Although the grin of the toothless guitar royally resting on a small strip of red carpet was one we woke up to every morning, like me, no one spoke about it. It stood leaning against our wooden kitchen scheme, which was itself precariously held together by fewer than three nails and kept erect by what remained in the wood's cellular memory from when it used to be a tree. No one who, as they used to say, knew what was good for them, dared bring up with my mother the subject of the guitar or its original owner.

There was a loud unspoken pact between my mother's friends and customers to keep silent about the guitar. In order to achieve the near impossible, double exploit of keeping her mind off the guitar while earning a living, Sis' Ncedi, my mother, had started operating a casino out of the capsule we called home. I guess casino is an elaborate but suitable term to describe a place where women and men congregated with the sole purpose of winning, but most likely losing, a little money.

They came. All sorts. They came to make sacrifices to gods with unspeakable names. But, for their sorrows and joys alike, they offered libations to each other under the pretext of offering these to their gods. Yoked to each other, they massed to help lug the crosses lassoed around their necks, the weight of which seemed to them lighter when carried as a shared burden.

I used to watch them from the vantage point of my Rockmobile. I would study their faces and tell myself stories about them. That was the only way I got to know them. None of them ever spoke to me. To them I was in every sense as good as everything Ncedi owned: there, but not fully functional and thus not worthy of any serious attention.

In our capsule, mind travel rapidly became my favourite pastime and the most entertaining reprieve from the punishing disregard I felt myself treated with. Seeing as it was difficult for me to physically move myself from one place to another, I resolved very early on that

I would not keep my thoughts imprisoned in this body that seldom travelled further than the distance to my school.

My favourite destination had become any place where I could sneak a peek at human interaction outside my own home. From time to time my imagination transported me from the faces of my mother's co-gamblers to their homes, where I could create in my mind's eye fantasies about what they had had, or had not had, for breakfast. I would imagine whom they had woken up next to that morning. I would imagine whom it was they went back home to account to on those days when they had lost at cards. But also I would imagine on whose faces the smiles would land on the very rare occasion when they had won. As a result, people's faces had a way of engraving themselves on my mind. And I became one of those people who could confidently state without fear of being proven wrong that I never forgot a face. That is how I came to know all my mother's regulars by face only.

One of my favourite faces was a man I had secretly christened The Glove. In my world real names did not have much currency. I figured that, since no one knew mine, there was little point in my knowing anyone else's, except for those that circumstance demanded that I knew. The Glove, to me, looked like a decrepit glove which had once belonged to a boxer who had never won a match in his life. He had what the kids in our neighbourhood called *skhumba* touch – a variation of scurvy that not only attached itself to his skin but to his personality and clothes as well.

My gift for remembering faces was useful for purposes of spotting newcomers, a service which I offered my mother for free. For her it was important because she used it to hustle those whose defences had not been solidly built up yet. We also kept a close eye on anyone new, and treated him or her with lavish suspicion until they proved themselves differently. This is why, on this Thursday, I could not release my gaze from the picture of the bizarre that was gradually taking shape right in front of my eyes. Even in my transfixion I could sense a lingering feeling that I had seen this apparition before. Perhaps not in this life, but seen it I had.

It was wearing a purple hat with two quail feathers on either side, and a brown corduroy jacket that looked as if it had not been washed since 1994. Right before my eyes, the figure changed from resembling a man to resembling a woman with such speed I could not keep up. My mind set about in a frantic hunt for clues and started with the most apparent offender: the corduroy jacket. From where I was sitting it looked very masculine, with a distinctly feminine feel about it, perhaps the shoulder pads. But, then again, poor people never make much of a fuss about the gender of their clothing.

The figure's bottom half was clad in a slick pair of pants, the type that I suspect would have been just the thing to be seen in on the streets of Sophiatown. The shoes were the obligatory brown and white two-toned type, the kind a pair of pants like that clearly wanted to rest its turn-ups on. From where I was sitting, the shoes appeared two sizes smaller than a regular man's. They were the only part of the apparel that was still intact. To complete the picture, there hung on its face a pair of goggles that looked as if they had sprung straight out of a 1960s fashion catalogue.

After much mental struggle about the figure's sex, I decided, based solely on how it walked – a swanky rhythmic right heel forward, right shoulder back, a shuffle-like drag of the left foot forward, and a jive-like twist of the left shoulder forward – that it was a man. I decided to hold onto this conviction until my mind and I had gathered more evidence to the contrary.

As he advanced, I saw he was clasping a bouquet of yellow roses, which would have been adorable had he not suffocated them to death on his way over. Perhaps they were even dead when he got them.

He surprised me by walking straight towards me. He surprised me even more when he squatted next to my Rockmobile and opened his mouth to speak. To me! No one except for my mother and Malum' Justice had spoken to me in six years. It was confirmed in my head at that point that he was a newcomer. It was only they that made the odd mistake of actually speaking to me.

I lie.

There was also the praying mantis that had taken up residence in our straw broom. Though, technically speaking, insects don't count as people, still she spoke to me. If truth be told, for truth always demands permission before it is told, maybe the mantis spoke more about me than to me. She would clasp her hands, focus her gaze to the sky and speak to someone she referred to as Gold. She would go into these long conversations with this person, Gold, who seemed to me to live some place beyond the clouds. It was in the way that the mantis spoke that I developed this suspicion. There was something in the mantis's voice that suggested, despite its skyward-facing posture, that it was really a place beyond the sky that she wanted her words to reach to. I concluded that this is where this Gold person must live.

They were mostly about me, these conversations. For instance, the mantis would say, "Ohhhh Gold, please guarantee this child a golden future," or "Ohhhh Gold, if only you would help her walk again!" I had grown to believe that this Gold person was either hard of hearing or just did not care. Hard of hearing, because everyone I had heard speak to him found it necessary to do so at the top of their voice. My mother, too, on the occasions when she spoke to him, did not care because he never responded to any of the requests either my mother or the mantis had placed before him. I personally thought it would make much more sense if Goldie relocated from that place on the other side of the sky to some place more pragmatic like, say, the Carlton Centre. Although we would still have to pay to speak to him, as we do in church, at least this time he would be much closer to us and thus better able to hear. And perhaps those who spoke to him would give up the need to shout when they addressed themselves to him.

All the same, I found the mantis a good companion and a very unobtrusive babysitter. The best of its kind with minimum demands – no payment, no unemployment insurance, just board and lodging. At this thought, I began to wonder about something else. I wondered how many mantises lived in the northern suburbs of Johannesburg, subsisting on prayer, board and lodging. My mind then hopped to Mevrou Zootvlei, Sis' Ntokozo's madam. Before she became our maestro.

Mevrou Zootvlei, I am not even sure if that was her real name. OohMmedem is what Sis' Ntokozo called her. *Ag tog*, but she was sweet, just never paid attention to detail. Never paid anyone anything, really. I remember her once saying, a couple of months after Sis' Ntokozo fell sick, "Ag, Nothokozo, man, according to me, I think it would be much easier and cheaper, man, for almal jinne, if you came and lived with us." The funny thing is that in the eight years we have lived next door to Bra Phandi and Sis' Ntokozo, I had come to believe that the woman's name was Ntokozo. But white people are funny that way and never hesitate to call you whatever their tongues can muster. I was in the middle of wondering what my name would sound like rolling off a white person's tongue – that's if they cared enough to say it. In my head I was playing around with and fumbling for variations of the pronunciation of my name, every time trying for things that sounded a bit, but not quite, like my real name. Zimbabushiso, perhaps?

My train of thought was interrupted by the sound of the apparition's voice …

"Zibusiso," he said, in a voice that sounded distinctly like a woman's. "So this is where you and Ncedi have been hiding all these years. Is she here?"

Caught in a moment of shock, I could not answer for a while, my silence possibly confirming in his head that physically disabled people are also mentally challenged. He spoke again, this time more slowly. Only at this point I was beginning to change my mind about him. He was increasingly becoming both in demeanour and decorum more and more a woman. My mind and I almost agreed that he was a she.

"Zibusiso, is your mother home?"

I had to quickly swallow the Zambezi River of saliva that was jamming my throat before I responded.

"She's not back from church yet, but she should be back any moment now." I said, trying to suppress the quiver in my voice.

"Is it okay if I wait in here for a while, until she comes back?" she asked. Her tender voice and her soft eyes, which I had stolen a glance at the second she took off her goggles, brought my mind and me into total agreement. She was a she. I nodded in response to her question. She grabbed an empty crate of beer that was standing next to the guitar, then froze for a moment, as if she and the guitar were being re-acquainted. I could swear, although at this point I was certain of precious little, that the guitar actually nodded to acknowledge her presence.

Zibusiso! She knew my name! Oh, how I so wanted to ask her how she knew my name. No one knew my name. I was Ncedi's daughter, or someone whose name was never uttered.

"I see she kept the guitar," she said, half muttering to herself, half speaking to me.

"We've had it for a very long time," I said, even though I was not sure she had wanted an answer. "One day when I start my Rock and Roll band, I will play it," I said, as my mother walked in.

"Now, child, who are you talking to?" My mother had not finished asking when the answer to that question nervously sprang from the beer crate it had been sitting on.

"Ncedi!" it said.

"Dan! Danisile, is that you?" My mother walked up to her answer and gave it a hug.

For a moment it felt as if time's pattern were disturbed. In each others' embrace, the past kissed the future and the present didn't seem to mind. That was one version of the truth. The kind I preferred. One that I also inferred circumstance had forced Ncedi and Danisile to ignore.

"Shooo, Dan!" my mother said repeatedly, sounding like someone trying to dislodge herself from a trance. Her jaw shook hands with her neck and caused a river of tears to well up in her eyes.

"I thought they said …" my mother said.

"Yes, I know, but I'm not," Dan interrupted her.

"But they said ... they said they had papers to prove it," Ncedi said.

"They said a lot of things, I know. But, as you can see, I am not. It wasn't true. Just like the many things they said about you," Dan said and extended her arm to give my mother the wilted roses.

Right there in the middle of the casino with all her sympathisers looking on, my mother's well of joy stole its first drop from a passing cloud. My mother and Dan stood looking at each other, oblivious of time and everyone in the room. They continued their conversation, which from the looks of it did not need a great quantity of words to keep it moving.

As an observer, I was not too sure what they were talking about, but they knew, and that for me was somehow enough. The smile I saw on my mother's face was also reassurance that whatever was being said was good news. She wore a hearty smile, a kind I had not seen on her since I lost my legs.

In spite of most of the conversation being lost to me, there were at least three graspable things I thought I heard said. The first was by my mother when she said to Dan, "Come sit outside, it's quieter there. You have so much to tell me."

The second was Dan's jack-in-the-just-opened-box question, "Do you still play?"

There was no verbal response to this question. Perhaps feeling ashamed, my mother nodded yes, or honestly shook her head for a no. I will never know. My mother is the one always telling me not to enter the business of old people, so for a spell I was satisfied with hearing just what I heard.

The next thing I heard was said at three minutes before a Soweto sunset, when those who owned TV sets prepared themselves for a daily dose of *Days of Our Lives*, and those who didn't contemplated theirs.

They spoke for a while afterwards, things that my ears were too lazy to grasp.

"You haven't done too badly for yourself, Ncedi," Dan said, as she got up, getting ready to say her goodbyes.

"Not exactly what I dreamt of, but at least I have a place to call home," was my mother's part abashed, part proud response.

A moment of silence passed without a word from either one of them. In that moment, in search of activity to keep my mind occupied, I caught a glimpse of the most orange sun setting. I heard the sands hissing their way through countless hourglasses in the horizon. I spied on the praying mantis peeping from under the broom in a way I had seen Sis' Ntokozo do on occasions when she felt too embarrassed to ask for a cup of mealie meal. I saw a green fly dallying with a decision to finish its journey. Then it finally decided on Danisile's lips as its target, more as an act of conspiring to give her an excuse to say something than as a preference. When the fly landed on Dan's lips, they both laughed and broke their silence.

"I see you kept it," Dan said, using her head to point to the guitar. This time she was not muttering. My mother gave a verbal response, sparing my now curious neck from straining in my attempt to enter old people's business.

"I did. It was the only thing I had that held memories of you."

Malum' Justice walked in from one of his sessions with the neighbourhood's meshugga intellectuals, as my mother called them; *amadod'ane* public opinion, as they called themselves.

"Ya, man! I knew the story was too good to be true!" Malum' Justice exclaimed on seeing Danisile.

The puzzle was slowly coming together in my head. The biggest piece was the smile missing in the tooth department, which Danisile flashed Malum' Justice to acknowledge his elation. That must have been the reason why my mother never bothered to restring the guitar after the last string snapped under the pressure of my fingers during one of my overly enthusiastic strumming sessions.

"I take it this means we will eventually be restringing that thing, then, Ncedi?" Malum' Justice said, motioning to the guitar and throwing the newspaper, which he had been squeezing under his armpit, on to his roll-away bed.

We all laughed. I must admit, however, that I was not too sure why I was laughing. What I do know, though, is that at that moment joy snuck in through our back door and left an endless supply of happiness for us.

From what I could make out from the rest of the conversation between my uncle, Dan and my mother, it seemed that over the years everyone had convinced themselves that Dan had died in exile. Those who were not convinced had forced themselves to kill her in their minds. My mother belonged to that latter group.

In truth, Dan had been roaming the streets of countries whose names I had never heard before, and now stood resurrected in our capsule.

"No one helps the dead," she finally said to stop Malum' Justice from assailing her with his million questions.

After supper Dan stood up again and announced her intention of leaving. But before she did, she again took my mother into her arms and gave her a passionate kiss, as if no one else was in the room. She also took the liberty of releasing the tears her eyes had been holding back since the moment she walked into our house. She thanked us for the meal, pinched my cheek and winked at me, and then patted Malum' Justice on the back.

"Where will you go?" my mother asked.

"My father's house has many houses. I'm sure there's a spot somewhere in this world I can call home."

"How about your people? Where is your brother?" Malum' Justice quizzed her.

"They said not to return to them unless I was married to a man, any man. So I guess on my own it will have to be for the longest time," Dan chimed.

"Stay the night, at least. Besides, it is way too late for you to start looking for a place now," Ncedi offered her kissing friend.

Dan stayed the night and infinite others afterwards. She restrung the guitar and taught me to play every song she herself knew how to, plus the many new ones we made up together. She became my partner in the pursuit of dreams. In between playing songs, we both indulged in our shared favourite pastime: mind travel. I introduced her to the praying mantis, who let it slip that now that her prayers had been answered, she might not be around for much longer.

Months went by. The mantis stopped its conversations with Gold. Music danced through our home. Malum' Justice found a job as a court interpreter. In a game of musical chairs, we had swapped positions with our neighbours. It was they who now threatened to sue us, because of the joyous racket that was known to spill through the cracks of our shack home.

We still did not have much by way of amplitude. The extra money that Malum' Justice made paid for our meals and firewood.

It was warmer in our hearth. It was warmer in our hearts, too, if truth be told, and this is the variety that is difficult to admit to. It did not hurt as much any more when the kids called me Rock. I had concluded that every rock star needed a stage name, and seeing as I was fast becoming one I reasoned what better name for a rock legend in the making to have than the name Rock?

GLOSSARY

A glossary is provided for instances where non-English words and phrases are not glossed in the story or where the meaning is not clarified through context.

A

Abaya: traditionally black, a long over/outer garment that covers the whole body.

Almal jinne: all of you.

Asante sana: thank you very much.

B

Batswana: the name of the people from which the country name, Botswana, is derived.

Bergies: homeless people who live in Cape Town, literally mountain people.

Beskuit: hard, dry biscuits, rusks.

Biltong: dried meat, jerky.

Bliksem: (slang) scoundrel.

Buibui: black cloth worn by women as a shawl.

D

Dominee: father, clergyman.

Donnered: (slang) beaten up.
Dool: board game.

H

Hakuna matata: no worries.
Hijab: head covering, traditionally worn by Muslim women.

K

Kabaka: king.
Kak: (vulgar) shit, crap.
Kanzu: a long garment, usually white, worn by men in East Africa.
Karibu: welcome.
Karibu tena nyumbani: welcome home again.
Koeksisters: plaited doughnut dipped in syrup.
Kwepena: game played by girls.

L

Lala salama: sleep well, goodnight.
Leteisi/mateisi: dresses made from German-print fabric, typically worn during traditional ceremonies.

M

Makwerekwere: (slang, often derogatory) foreigner, illegal immigrant.
Mampoer: home-made peach brandy.
Mampo vipi: hey what's up? how are you doing? how are things?
Mandazi: an East African doughnut.
Moegoe: (slang, derogatory) idiot, stupid person.
Moer: (slang) beat up, kill.
Moffies: a derogatory term for homosexuals, queers.
Motswana: singular of Batswana.

N

Nachtmaal (or Nagmaal): holy communion.

Nooit: never, often used to express "You don't say!" or "Would I lie to you!"

O

Ouderling: elder.

P

Piel: penis.

Pikipiki: motorcycle.

Poort: gateway, narrow mountain pass.

S

Sadza: stiff mealie meal porridge, often eaten with barbequed meat.

Salama: wellbeing, peace.

Skelms: crooks, rogues.

Z

Zol: spliff, joint, marijuana cigarette.

AUTHOR BIOGRAPHIES

BARBARA ADAIR

Barbara Adair has published two novels. *In Tangier We Killed the Blue Parrot* (2004), set in Morocco in the 1950s and based loosely on the life of Paul Bowles and Jane Bowles, was shortlisted for the Sunday Times Literary Award in 2006. *End* (2007) generated debate about the artificiality of novel writing, gender roles and postmodernism in the South African context. It was shortlisted for the African regional prize of the Commonwealth Book Prize in 2008. Adair also writes travel essays.

MONICA ARAC DE NYEKO

Monica Arac de Nyeko is a Ugandan writer of fiction. Her story "Jambula Tree" was the winner of the Caine Prize in 2007. She studied at Makerere University and the University of Groningen.

RICHARD DE NOOY

Richard de Nooy (1965) grew up in Johannesburg, but has lived in Amsterdam for more than 25 years. He writes his novels in English and Dutch. His first novel, *Six Fang Marks and a Tetanus Shot* (Jacana, 2007), won the University of Johannesburg Prize for Best First Book. It was published in Dutch as *Zes beetwonden en een tetanusprik* by Nijgh & Van Ditmar in 2008. De Nooy received a grant from the Dutch Foundation for Literature to write his second novel in Dutch. *Zacht als Staal* (Nijgh & Van Ditmar, 2010) was long-listed for the prestigious AKO Literatuurprijs. The English edition, *The Big Stick*, was published in South Africa by Jacana in 2012. De Nooy's third novel, *Zendingsdrang*, was published in Dutch by Nijgh & Van Ditmar in 2013. The English edition, *The Unsaid*, is expected to be released later this year.

ROGER DIAMOND

Born in Cape Town, Roger Diamond studied geology at the University of Cape Town. He now does environmental work and leads outreach and conservation activities for the Mountain Club of South Africa. One of his stories was published in *Yes, I Am! Writing by South African Gay Men.*

NATASHA DISTILLER

Natasha Distiller was, until recently, Associate Professor of English at the University of Cape Town. She remains a Research Associate of the Institute for the Humanities in Africa at UCT. She has published a number of books, short stories and academic articles, among them *Fixing Gender: lesbian mothers and the Oedipus complex* (Farleigh Dickinson University Press 2011) and *Shakespeare and the Coconuts: on post-apartheid South African culture* (Wits University Press 2012). She currently lives in Berkeley, California, with her wife and two children, where she is working in the LGBTQ movement and studying clinical psychology. She continues to write and publish.

K. SELLO DUIKER

K. Sello Duiker was born in 1974 and grew up in Soweto and East London. He studied at Rhodes University where, with a few friends, he started a poetry society called Seeds. A course called "English in Africa", which dealt with African writers, made a great impression on him, and he was also influenced in that time by the Eastern Cape as the birthplace of a generation of black intellectuals. After graduating with majors in journalism and art history, he moved to Cape Town, and it is there that he found his writing voice. Duiker studied copywriting and went on to work as an advertising copywriter, a television scriptwriter and later as commissioning editor for the South African Broadcasting Corporation. His first novel, *Thirteen Cents*, an extract from which is published here, won the African regional prize in the 2001 Commonwealth Book Prize. Published the same year, *The Quiet Violence of Dreams* was awarded the 2001 Herman Charles Bosman Prize for English Literature. Duiker often said that his mother, an insatiable reader, inspired his decision to become a writer. He died in 2005.

MARTIN HATCHUEL

Martin Hatchuel feels a strong affinity for the Eastern Cape Province, and is particularly interested in the South African War of 1899–1902.

ANNIE HOLMES

Annie Holmes is a Zimbabwean writer, editor and filmmaker. Her short fiction has been published in *Lip from Southern African Women*, *Writing Still: New Stories from Zimbabwe*, *Women Writing Zimbabwe* and *Cimarron Review*. Her story "Can you Hear Me Now?" was nominated for a Pushcart Prize in 2007. The Canadian journal *Public* commissioned her to write a short memoir of Zimbabwean independence, *Good Red*, and she was awarded a 2012 writing residency at Hedgebrook. With fiction writer Peter Orner, Annie co-edited a collection of Zimbabwean narratives in McSweeney's Voice of Witness series, published in the US as *Hope Deferred* and in South Africa by Jonathan Ball under the title *Don't Listen to What I'm About to Say*. She studied in Cape Town, Johannesburg and San Francisco and now lives in London, UK.

BEATRICE LAMWAKA

Beatrice Lamwaka is the general secretary of the Ugandan Women's Writers Association (FEMRITE). She was a finalist for the PEN/Studzinski Literary Award in 2009 and a fellow in the Harry Frank Guggenheim Foundation/African Institute of South Africa Young Scholars programme in 2009. She is the author of *Anena's Victory*, a supplementary reader in primary schools. Her short stories have been published in literary journals and anthologies. Lamwaka is working on her first novel, *Beyond My World*, and a collection of short stories, *The Garden of Mushrooms*. Lamwaka was shortlisted for the 2011 Caine Prize for African Writing.

KAREN MARTIN

Karen Martin is a fiction writer, collage artist and professional editor. In 2010, she published her first stories in *ITCH*, a South African-based multimedia online journal. In 2011, she was awarded a fellowship to Syracuse University's three-year creative writing MFA program. In 2012, she was artist-in-residence at the Norman Mailer Writers Colony and the Woodstock Byrdcliffe Guild. In 2013, she was awarded the Allen and Nirelle Galson Prize for Fiction by *Stone Canoe*, a journal that showcases artists and writers with ties to Upstate New York. Karen has initiated and developed several projects for GALA, including *Balancing Act,* a book and exhibition of South African LGBTI youth life stories, and *Till the Time of Trial*, a booklet featuring the prison letters of LGBTI and HIV/AIDS activist Simon Nkoli. She is the co-editor of *Sex and Politics*, a collection of essays, memoirs and archival documents about the South African LGBTI rights movement and the anti-apartheid struggle. She is a member of the GALA board of trustees.

WAMUWI MBAO

Wamuwi Mbao is a Zambian scholar of literature and critical theory at the University of Stellenbosch. His short story "The Limited Circle is Pure", a snapshot of life in suburban South Africa, was published in the fourth *Laugh It Off* annual, and his short story "The Obvious Child" was published in *Sharp!*

MERCY MINAH

Mercy Minah is a pseudonym. The author, who lives in Johannesburg, is not out to her family, and the pseudonym allows her to publish without the risk of being discovered by them. Mercy is a feminist and an aspiring queer author, poet and activist. She identifies as a queer, gender-nonconfoming artist, and says, "My family is staunchly religious and they don't approve of homosexuality or most of my views and opinions about the world. It's easier not to come out to them under these circumstances, particularly because I still live with my mother and am still dependent on her, for food and a roof over my head. I write poetry, short stories and songs that are centred on my queer identity, constantly. I draw sometimes as well. I would like to be incredibly successful someday as a writer-actress-singer-poet-activist. I'm studying law as a means of achieving my goal of being a human rights activist and working for the UN some day. I dream, a lot."

TO MOLEFE

To Molefe is a creative writing student at the University of Cape Town, and a freelance writer and editor. His thesis, which he hopes will become his first novel, is currently the greatest love and hate of his life.

WAME MOLEFHE

Wame Molefhe was born in Francistown, Botswana, and has lived most of her life in Gaborone. *Just Once*, a collection of short stories for children, was published in 2009, and her other stories have appeared in anthologies and journals. *Go Tell the Sun*, a collection of short fiction, was published by Modjaji Books in 2011. She also writes travel articles, and she has written for television documentaries and for radio.

LINDIWE NKUTHA

Lindiwe Nkutha is a poet, storyteller and filmmaker born in Soweto and based in South Africa. Trained as an accountant and now working as a business development consultant, Nkutha has come to heed the messages she has heard life whisper into her eyes and ears. She has acquired skills in photography and videography to complement her vocation to tell stories. Some of her poetry has been published in feminist publications in the Southern Africa Development Community region and read on the stages of Johannesburg's underground poetry scene. Her short film, *Muted Screams,* was shown in South Africa and the UK. Nkutha has showcased two debut pieces of photographic work as part of the Female Activation through Creative Empowerment–Ansisters constellation: a photographic exhibition and a multimedia, polyphonous narrative, with characters drawn from archetypes across cultures and different time periods.

DAVINA OWOMBRE

Davina Owombre lives in Abuja, Nigeria. Her story "Sarah" was published in the anthology of erotic fiction *See You Next Tuesday: The Second Coming* in 2008.

EMIL RORKE

Emil Rorke was born in Zimbabwe. He described himself as an aspirant writer, screenwriter, philosopher, poet and Zen monk (though too profane to be one) at the age of 60 when he submitted "Poisoned Grief" to this anthology. He died in 2010.

DOLAR VASANI

Dolar Vasani is Indian with Ugandan roots. Her family relocated to the UK in 1972, following Idi Amin's expulsion of Indian Ugandans. Since the early 1990s she has pursued a career in international development, based in Southern and East Africa. Living in Tanzania with her partner has been Vasani's source of inspiration for exploring erotic lesbian fiction. She is currently working on her book, *12 Flashes*.

RAHIEM WHISGARY

Born and raised in Johannesburg, Rahiem Whisgary is a dramatic arts graduate of the University of the Witwatersrand with an interest in writing, physical theatre and performance art. Whisgary's story, "Aadil", was published in the collection *Yes, I Am! Writing by South African Gay Men*. In 2010, he performed in Bailey Snyman's *Outside* at the Barney Simon Theatre as part of the FNB Dance Umbrella and in Kabi Thulo's *Tsela* as part of the WALE festival.

MAKHOSAZANA XABA

Makhosazana Xaba is a former writing fellow at the Wits Institute for Social and Economic Research (WISER) and is currently a writing fellow at the Wits School of Public Health. She is the author of two poetry collections: *these hands* (2005) and *Tongues of their Mothers* (2008). Her forthcoming début collection of short fiction, *Running and other stories*, will be published by Modjadji Books. She is the winner of the 2005 Deon Hofmeyr Award for Creative Writing and holds an MA in Writing from the University of the Witwatersrand.

ACKNOWLEDGEMENTS

We want to express our appreciation to our talented editors, Karen Martin and Makhosazana Xaba, who saw this project to completion in spite of challenges posed by multiple commitments, geographic distance, and production delays. Their vision, perseverance, and sacrifices have helped make this book the best that it can be.

To the staff of Gay and Lesbian Memory in Action, thank you for the many ways each of you contributed to this book. In particular, we acknowledge Anthony Manion, who commissioned this book and oversaw its development, and John Marnell, who helped bring it to completion.

Special thanks go to Colleen Higgs, our publisher at MaThoko's Books, for her editorial and other insights and ongoing encouragement, and to copyeditor Gill Gimberg for the eagle eye she brought to the text, and her hard work and patience in clearing the permissions and compiling the authors' biographies. Thanks also go to Carla Kreuser for the artistic flair that she brought to the design of the cover.

We also owe an enormous debt to Pumla Dineo Gqola, whose excellent introduction to the book goes far beyond what we had any reason to expect.

We cannot end without giving special acknowledgement to the authors who have so generously contributed their work to this book, and without whom it would not exist. Sadly, Emil Rorke passed away before he could see his story, "Poisoned Grief", published, and we send our condolences to Emil's family on their loss. Some of the stories in this collection have been published previously and we would like to thank the publishers: *Thirteen Cents*, K. Sello Duiker, New Africa Books, 2000; *Go Tell the Sun*, Wame Molefhe, Modjaji Books, 2011; *The Big Stick*, Richard de Nooy, Jacana Media, 2011.

Some of the stories have previously appeared in the following publications: "Asking for It", Natasha Distiller, *Urban 03: Collected New South African Short Stories*, Spearhead, New Africa Books, 2003; "Pinch", Martin Hatchuel, *African PENS 2011: New Writing From Southern Africa*, Jacana Media, 2011; "Rock", Lindiwe Nkutha, *African Road: New Writing from Southern Africa 2006*, Spearhead, New Africa Books, 2006; "Jambula Tree", Monica Arac de Nyeko, *Jambula Tree and Other Stories: The Caine Prize for African Writing 8th Annual Collection*, Jacana Media, 2008.

The publication of this book was made possible by core support from The Atlantic Philanthropies.

– GAY AND LESBIAN MEMORY IN ACTION (GALA)